THE MISADVENTURES
OF AN IMPERFECT WOMAN

the **MISADVENTURES** of an
IMPERFECT WOMAN

BELA GARY

Stardustings Press
www.stardustings.com

Published by Stardustings Press
PO Box 9532
Chapel Hill, NC 27515
www.stardustings.com

Printed in the United States of America

LCCN: 2023939645
ISBN: 978-1-7363797-1-4

*To the courageous souls who have faced
difficult challenges on their journey.
Through consciously embracing love and forgiveness,
towards others and yourself, you embark on a
path of transformation and healing.*

ACKNOWLEDGMENTS

Thank you to my amazing family and friends for your love and support. This book took way too long to complete. Although most of it was written in my head, I didn't feel the need to put pen to paper until the fall of 2022. Everything happens in divine timing.

I'm grateful to have found a home in the realm of visionary and spiritual fiction. Some insist on calling it speculative or metaphysical. Not me.

I believe in everything.

In order to heal we must first forgive…
And sometimes that person we
must forgive is ourselves.

–Mia Bron

THERE IS ONLY ME

I regret everything—every decision I've made, every leap of faith I've taken. It all ended in disaster. "Trust your intuition," they said. "Go with the flow," they urged. "Follow your heart." My heart has led me into a quagmire of despair. I am stuck in muddy quicksand, and the more I try to escape, the deeper I sink. I'm afraid I'll eventually be buried and stay forever submerged in obscurity, in the same place, day after day, life after life, as everyone dances, and new life grows above me. I want to rejoin the living. I plead and beg for help. Who will dig me out? But I can only watch the dancers, because I am unable to speak. My mouth is full of mud. I don't understand how I'm still breathing. I watch—they grow old with grace and in stable companionship, and I grow sickly and ancient in turmoil and solitude.

Sometimes faith makes no difference. Positive thinking is naïve and unrealistic, a way to escape reality. It's a childlike belief that wishes come true. All the positive thinking in the world can't stop death or pain or change the outcome. I used to think differently. I used to think I could make wishes, that love made a difference. I would change the world! I believed I could fix anything and everything. We would be together, as we were supposed to be. It was a crazy idea. The more I read and researched, the more I believed that my faith would make a difference. If only I believed in it hard enough, it would come to pass. I trusted the Universe, God…whatever I believed existed. I was living in a fantasy land. I'd been deceived. No—I'd deceived myself. What I'd believed to be magic and fate was simply toxicity and poor choices.

What if I hadn't tried hard enough? What if I didn't have enough faith? Is that why I'd failed?

No. I had to stop myself from thinking these thoughts. That's the way I used to think. That was the old me—faith, trust, and pixie dust. Now I know bad things happen in our lives over which we have no control. We can't always have those things we wish for—even if we feel we are supposed to have them. Faith and hope are irrelevant. I'm not special. Life is not about having any special purpose or even about love. Life is trial after trial. In surviving those trials and facing the challenges, we grow strong and become self-reliant. Unless I accepted that, I would be forever stuck in false hope. You cannot prevent the bad and manifest the good. You can't prevent life. The notion that you can manifest your heart's desire is a lie. Life is pain. And faith in yourself is the only real faith. Faith that you can deal with tragedies and become a survivor. You need to flow with the pain. If you wallow, you stop living. Let it go.

But I couldn't move. I couldn't let it go. Rationally, I knew what I needed to do. Emotionally, I couldn't erase the memories or the pain. What else do I need to do? I've done it all. I've healed. Why is he still part of me?

Finally, I did it. I erased the images and squashed the pain. I refused to think about it. I slowly tunneled my way out of the darkness, spewing mud from my mouth, finally breathing easily. I was free, not through faith or God, but through sheer strength and firm free will.

PHOENIX

I rose from the mud, strong and ready to move forward. I was propelled by an initial sense of freedom, and I'd finally found the courage to let go. I had held on to deep pain for too long. It had become part of me. I was afraid it would define how I moved through the rest of my life. So I burned my past self, walking away from the ashes and soaring into the light. I believed with all my soul that I had been reborn.

DO YOU REALLY
WANT TO KNOW?

———◆———

"I can talk endlessly about it. When people ask me questions, I easily share all the details. Does it make me feel better? I'm not sure. It was supposed to help me heal. In human terms, it's not even an important story. I didn't change the world. I didn't deeply impact the lives of others. In fact, I never let on to anyone how difficult it was for me. I was alone in the shadows but pretending I was love and light. Appearing perfect on the outside, while inside I was refereeing a battle between my heart and mind.

"Is it about growth? Yes—everything we survive brings growth. There are already too many stories about growth and evolution, inspirational stories with deeply admired and pitied survivors. I don't want to be just another survivor. We've become a world of over-sharers. That's why I'm only sharing my story with you."

I paused. He looked at me, anticipating what I would say next.

"My story isn't about anything monumental. It's trivial, especially when you look at the hate and chaos in the world, not just now but throughout history. I don't believe things are worse now than they were before. I think it's simply because people are finally waking up and seeing into the darkness and wanting to bring forth the light. That doesn't diminish the importance of my story, though.

"My story is about everything. Hope. Love. Balance. Pain. Obsession. The past. The future. See? My story is a creation of my reality—the world of pain and love I designed for myself. From my perspective. It's a story about life.

"I've already told you the other story. This could be a continuation of that story or an entirely different story. There are limitless possible stories. I chose this one because I followed an unconventional path. My brokenness influenced my choices, and those choices impacted my entire life. Perhaps it's the story of understanding why."

DIVING IN

Just a few short weeks after our initial breakup, I dove into dating again. I didn't feel it was too soon. I wanted to move on, and I felt I was ready. The deep love and resulting loss had impacted me profoundly, surprising me with its intensity and grief. But I was determined to let it go. I was tired of being home, tired of trying to find ways to keep busy, and tired of feeling stuck in sadness and regret.

I'm better than that, I told myself.

So I jumped back in, not wanting to waste any more time. I wasn't the type of person who could grieve for very long. Grief prevents joy, and life is about joy. Life is too short.

Several failed dates later—I grew frustrated. I told myself, *Calm down.*

Looking at my statistics in dating, I had one success for every ten failures. Success only meant that I liked the man enough to go on a second date. What happened after the second date was… unpredictable. I hadn't made it past that point with anyone. I was newly divorced and had just started dating around the time I met *him*. I had still been figuring out what I wanted in a man. The only thing I knew was that I wanted a man and that the search was thoroughly enjoyable. I was a kid in a candy shop.

After our breakup, all of that changed. It was more difficult dating, and everything moved excruciatingly slowly. I had swiped through all the men on some dating apps—

mostly left-swipes. I tried different apps, but it was all the same men, and some had been on several apps for a while. I wondered why they were still single.

Why am I still single?

Matching was a rare event, and very often those I matched with were boring or bizarre.

Then it finally happened. I found a man who seemed to fit the definition of what I wanted. I was attracted to him, plus he seemed a little bit rebellious and conveyed just enough mystery to pique my interest. He wasn't an ordinary man—unconventional and yet seemingly stable.

However, the desire for the unconventional and mysterious turned out to be a problem. We had our second date, and then a third, but there was far too much irregular behavior on his part. I soon grew annoyed and decided he wasn't worth my time.

None of them were.

BUOYED BY YOUR LOVE

Journal Entry

I am wading in the water, remaining in the shallows. Then I see you on the rocks, far offshore. Your light and beauty beckon me. I'm anxious, afraid of drowning. But you pull me toward you like a magnet. I am instinctively and uncontrollably drawn to you. I believe that drowning is impossible; I am buoyed by your love.

I dive in and swim out to you near the rocks. You stand on the rocky shore, looking down at your feet. You seem uncertain. I wonder if you are searching for clarity. Or are you gathering courage? I wait for you as I patiently tread water. The waves grow higher and wilder. I feel the current trying to pull me out to sea. I'm tired, and I don't think I can continue fighting the sea much longer. I only have two choices—wait patiently for you to dive in or climb on the rocks and convince you to take the plunge.

You turn your back to me just as a small sailboat appears. I don't have a choice. I need to get to calmer waters, or I'll drown. I climb aboard the sailboat and head toward you, hoping you will change your mind. As I approach, you start to walk away. I call your name, but you continue walking. My only option is to sail back to shore. Then I realize I have another option. I can sail to another cove. Maybe there I will find someone willing to swim in the water with me.

I unfurl my sails and look back at you one more time. You're no longer on the rocks. I turn my focus forward, sailing to a fresh beginning, hoping that the disappointment will lessen the farther I move away from you.

UNCONVENTIONAL

I wanted dating to be my salvation, a way to forget him. But I couldn't stop thinking about him. I was constantly comparing him to every man I met. I didn't feel anything at all comparable to what I'd felt for him. I felt little or no emotion for those men, no deep connection. I wanted to feel. I desperately tried to feel something. I created all sorts of stories in my mind about what *should* happen.

I will love you. I will live happily ever after.

As if my heart could respond on command. This period was just a small part of my life but seemed to last forever.

I should stop dating. There were just too many failures.

I sought out the unconventional, hoping that it would lead me to love, and ultimately, amnesia. Searching behind the mysterious exteriors of these unconventional men somehow became a challenge. Was I trying to tame them? To take away their mystery? Perhaps. I found that once I cleared away the mystery there was a deep darkness, a wrongness. A wrongness I knew already existed but denied intuitively knowing. I was probably trying to fix them, yet again. Find their darkness and give them light. And once I healed them, then what? They would love me?

I knew it had to stop. And the only way to stop was to stop dating until I was fully healed. However long it took. I had no idea—I just wanted to feel like myself again. Days were fine, weeks also, months—well, maybe. Years, no way. I would rather just live life as a broken person, maybe settling for a stable, inauthentic relationship. Giving up on love. I damn well wasn't going to stay away from dating for years. Who takes years to heal anyway? Someone weak. Not me.

It was a difficult decision. Dating kept me occupied. It eased my mind and my heart. I had tried very hard to stop thinking about him, but the thoughts just kept coming. The emotions, particularly the pain, increased as the thoughts consumed me. I would tell myself to stop without effect. But when I was dating, my mind was less cluttered. My thoughts of him were obscured, and I felt free. Clearing my mind ultimately helped lessen the pain in my heart—until I grew too attached.

I wished my father could've helped me. He had died a few years earlier, and I would speak to him often. He had been silent lately, almost as if he wanted me to figure things out on my own. I still spoke to him—sometimes out loud, asking him questions, sometimes stating facts. I needed help. I knew he was listening—I could feel his presence. It was all normal. Once I even saw his silhouette in my kitchen. He smiled at me. It was all normal. I smiled back and he disappeared.

I also clearly remember the first time he spoke to me after his death. I was shocked. I was struggling—in pain, lost in confusion from heartbreak—when suddenly, I heard his voice say, *I can't help you if you're sad.* I had thought, *What a strange thing to say.* Sadness is sadness. It exists, and ignoring it just traps the pain inside of you. What did he mean? I still wasn't sure, but I repeated the words in my head, sometimes forcing myself to stop being sad. I understood what he meant—that if you wallow in sadness and self-pity, you will be stuck in negativity. Nothing positive can happen if you have a low, negative vibration.

I needed him to say something, give me advice about dating. *What do I do?*

I waited. There was no reply. I was on my own.

Without dating, I was a mess. The problem was in dating, I was also a mess. Which was the worst mess?

Me, I am the worst mess.

They say you need to heal and take a break from dating after a breakup. I'd tried that several times, but in truth, those breaks were very short, lasting only a month or two. Maybe I needed more time. I decided to follow their advice. Again. I had nothing to lose that I hadn't already lost.

THE GOLDEN CHARIOT

Journal Entry

I was soaring through the sky in a golden chariot. No horses or reins, just an invisible guide who spoke to me telepathically. I recognized the speaker, but I couldn't remember who it was. It was a confident, strong, and omnipotent voice. I knew that voice. Who was it? As we traveled, I recognized the places. It was so clear, so vivid. It had to be a memory and not a dream. Was I awake? Was I remembering? I knew I had been there before, riding the chariot in the sky, being led by a powerful voice.

I flew through a forest filled with towering trees. Their tops stretched into space. It was dark but not menacing. There were many seemingly significant landmarks, but we moved quickly, and I only caught glimpses of a few scenes: a fortress, an old stone structure, and possibly a stone circle, unrecognizable but ancient. I emerged from the forest through a marked path in the sky. More artifacts. Ancient Roman ruins. The guide said something unintelligible. There was a partial understanding on my part. History. My history? I wasn't sure. Maybe the history of the world. Or maybe these were visions of my past lives.

My guide spoke other words, but they were gibberish. Although I couldn't understand, I could sense that the words were important, meant to explain some significant events that had taken place. Or maybe were still yet to be? I passed through other landscapes: a Greek temple, Atlantis, and a planet with two suns. There was so much more, but it all flashed by quickly.

Suddenly, to my right, I saw him. He was lying on the ground on top of a slab of concrete. Injured, maybe dead. I yelled at my guide to stop. I wanted to see him. However, the chariot veered left and picked up speed, moving quickly away from him.

"No," I pleaded. "Take me to him!"

"It's not for you. Not now," replied the voice, finally understandable.

While I was disappointed, in the dream I understood why. But when I woke up, I lost all sense of understanding. Only my dream self, perhaps my subconscious, possessed this inner knowledge. Only my dream self comprehended why I couldn't stop. I knew from experience that anything is possible in dreams. I could have forced the chariot to stop. I could have jumped off the chariot. In this dream, I didn't.

The chariot continued past wondrous places, a history, a viewing through time. It was beautiful and powerful, and yet, my focus was on him. I kept turning around, searching for him. He was all I wanted.

I'd tried to stop thinking about him. I was desperately trying to erase my desire for him, and yet the dreams came, weakening me. What did the dream mean? Was it the past or the future? A past life or future life? Or was it a different timeline entirely bleeding into my dreams? Maybe the dream was about understanding the path I needed to take, without him. He was no longer significant in my life, and I should leave the past in the past. That's what I kept telling myself, falsely convincing myself that my interpretation and present feelings were true.

A powerful dream. Significant. History, time travel, space. I was shown everything. And yet, all I could think about were the words, "He is not for you." But the guide had added, "Not now."

Not now or ever? I wondered what the guide meant. I hated hearing it. "Not now," brought a small ray of hope, more delusion. I decided "Not now" was a throwaway line. All I needed to know was that I was on a solitary journey. It was a large dose of reality.

I need to keep working on my book. It's taking far too long. But I can't write sometimes. The words make little sense and I'm tired of writing about love and loss.

IRONY

I was alone and happy enough. No men. I felt relieved, even though admittedly I was a bit lonely. I pushed the feelings of loneliness aside. At least I didn't have to go through the effort of shaving my legs anymore. No makeup, no thought given to clothes. It was pure relief not to dress up and play a role. It was winter, and I was cocooned in my warm home, only leaving to see friends, family, and the usual necessities of life.

I was enjoying my jump into solitude. It was a huge leap. I loved the old incessant pattern. Drinks, dinner, romance, sex. *Right.* There was hardly any romance. It seemed to be all about pleasure. Ego. Whatever it was, I was done. And happy. Enough. I would enjoy and savor everything life had to offer. Every moment would be beautiful and significant. I was more peaceful and balanced, heart and mind no longer arguing, the inner uncontrollable voice silenced. I had control over my life. No more men, no more false beliefs.

I had also accepted my fate. *I didn't need anything from a man.* I got everything I needed from those around me and my passions. I didn't long for a man anymore. Those were the silly desires of an immature woman. I decided to let my hair go gray. I imagined my long, silver—no, pure white—hair. The healer. The hermit. The mystical witch.

Why, then, did the Universe decide to throw me a curve ball, yet another challenge? Maybe the Universe was saving me. Deep down, I was still fearful to die old and alone. The Universe decided that it would speed things up, get it all over with, end it, finish it…so I could die young(ish) and alone instead. Just when I was finally accepting solitude and finding my way to emotional balance. Isn't that just like the Universe, throwing me yet another challenge?

I was surprisingly fine when I heard the news. I laughed, shocking the poor doctor who just looked at me as if I had lost my mind.

"Are you okay?" she asked, looking at me with deep concern on her face.

I stopped laughing and looked at her, still smiling.

"Yes. It's just funny because I'm finally happy. I don't need a man. I appreciate every moment of life and I try to live in the now. I'm grateful for many things," I answered, repeating the mantra I told myself every day.

"I guess it's irony," I whispered.

Was it irony? Or just bad luck? I kept thinking of Alanis Morrisette's song "Ironic," and how nothing she described in the song was ironic at all. Just circumstances and bad luck. But maybe that was the irony of the song.

I hated labeling things incorrectly. I pondered the meaning of irony. For several seconds, I was in a foggy state, analyzing the meaning of the word irony and how to use it in writing. No, this was not irony. Destiny maybe?

It doesn't matter.

I needed to stop the endless desire to connect the dots in my mind. I was in overdrive trying to label and identify the part of the language that would describe my tragedy. The idea of irony made it less serious. Irony is humorous, after all.

Thanks for the laughs, Universe.

"Are you okay?" the doctor asked again.

"Yes, I'm fine. Just processing," I replied.

I had a rare brain cancer, incurable, but they could prolong my life with chemo and other nasty-sounding treatments. I had made the decision a long time ago that I would never suffer like that unless the cure would one hundred percent get rid of my cancer without making my quality of life worse. I knew chemo did more harm than cancer itself. *No way.* I had seen it too many times with people I loved. Nope. I had already decided that if I ever found out I had cancer, I would just continue to live, making my remaining days as adventurous and joyful as possible. Inner peace with a touch of insanity, maybe?

I made up my mind, and I knew what to do. I was going to do all the crazy things I hadn't done yet, plus more of the ones I had already done and thoroughly enjoyed.

The doctor said many things I didn't pay attention to and handed me lots of written info. I shoved everything into my purse. I didn't want to think about it anymore.

I told no one. I didn't want people to worry about me or try to talk me out of my decision. I didn't want pity of any sort. Pity was uncomfortable. Being pitied by others made me feel weak.

I decided to quit my job and sell my house. I would put all my possessions in storage, telling everyone it was time for a big move and that I wanted freedom. I told everyone I was still healing from a broken heart, combined with a second midlife crisis, and I needed to protect my mental and spiritual health by making a radical life change.

Oh, that sounded so good.

And it was almost entirely true. The only part I left out was that I was dying.

I planned to travel for a bit and continue writing. Maybe I would have a fling or two with some fiery men. Maybe three. Or even more. Did it even matter how many at this point? I was dying. I was going to do all the stupid, impulsive things I had once feared. Impending death was an open invitation to not give a damn. I didn't care what people thought anymore. Maybe I would do things that would shock everyone. They would think I was destroying my life.

Guess what? It's already pretty much destroyed.

Almost over. And I was going to enjoy every bit of it.

THE INFLEXIBLE HEART

Before I found out that I was dying, I had finally achieved the balance I had craved for years. My heart and mind were no longer arguing. The heart felt and the mind accepted without trying to overthink and overrule. The mind thought without the heart feeling too deeply. This imbalance had always been my downfall in dating in the past. I was confident I could maintain the balance and progress forward in my life. I was relatively financially secure, I was passionate about my career, and I knew exactly what I wanted. At least in a general sense. I knew where I was going, although I didn't know, nor did I plan, how to get there. I was free to do what I wanted, make spontaneous decisions, and travel. I no longer clung to things that had little significance to me. All the trivial little things people think about—like men. I was done with it all. I had accepted my fate. I chose my friends, those who gave me joy and were aligned with my beliefs. I wasn't afraid to be different. I lived mostly in the real world but also balanced my spiritual self. No longer was I singularly obsessed with the Universe and magic. Harmony, equilibrium. Not too much spirituality, just enough to maintain the balance.

I was happy and stable.

I continued to say those words to myself after I found out I was dying. That I was happy and balanced. That I didn't need anything from anyone. That I could continue with that same balance as I enjoyed my last moments on earth. However, I lied. Something changed shortly after I heard I was dying. It was subtle at first, but a few days later, it overwhelmed me. And then it consumed me. Despite how much I fought against wanting it, it overtook my will. I needed to do something bigger. It became a quest. No, it wasn't the answer to the mysteries of the Universe. It was far more complicated than that.

I decided to search for the perfect man, a vision I had so clearly formed in my mind long ago. I had stopped searching because it was doing me more harm than good. But now, feeling free, I knew exactly what I needed to do. I didn't ask myself why or what was the point. I had nothing left to lose, and it sounded like a great way to spend the rest of my life. In the company of men. Only the best men.

THE LIST

I made a non-negotiable list. Those things that I would never compromise. My desires in a man, a vision of what he must be. The basic things. He must be giving, honest, loyal, fun, outgoing, confident, and passionate. Probably what every woman wants. The normal desires of many people. Of course, most of us are too messed up to identify those things in men we meet. We end up going to the other side of the spectrum and finding men with the opposite qualities. I knew I had to maintain my balance. I knew from experience I often lost myself and subsequently went into a *heart vs. mind* death spiral.

Some people settled for less. They would just take what they could get. I wondered if maybe the ones who settled were the normal and balanced ones. They lived happy lives of peace because they'd stopped searching for their perfect mate and they had no expectations. They settled.

Damn it. I'm not settling. It's all or nothing.

My non-negotiable list grew. Suddenly, I had over fifty non-negotiables. *Fifty.* They included things such as *He must love to dance. He must be a Democrat. He must have traveled all over the world.* Speak another language? That was a maybe—I was still thinking about whether to add it to my list. My *maybe* list included qualities I wanted but felt I was asking for too much if I included them. So many absurd traits and characteristics—*was this man a fantasy?*

How could anyone realistically satisfy my requirements? Later, I would question the picture I'd painted in my mind of the ideal man. But at that moment, I refused to settle for anything less.

I created a formula, a system of wading through the men. I went back to dating online but in a very precise and limited way. One swipe at a time, one man at a time, so I could focus my energy on determining if he was the perfect man. Multiple dating? I was done with that. Too much energy was wasted and scattered that way. I would ask a lot of questions before I decided whether that person was even worthy of meeting.

You are worthy, I would tell him. No, I wouldn't tell him that. That would give him too much confidence.

What do you do? Not that I cared about whether they had money or not, but what a person does for work tells you a lot about who they are and how they live their lives. It sounds obvious to say that, but I think I gave it more thought than some women might. While most women would jump at the chance to date a rich, powerful CEO, I would want to know what kind of business or company they ran. I couldn't date anyone who was the CEO of a company that exploited people or poisoned the environment. His work should embody a positive or creative cause. "I help kids…I started a foundation…I teach meditation…" I didn't care if he worked in a job some might see as being menial. He could be a tree cutter or a janitor as long as he was passionate about art, travel, or saving the world. I would be all-in if a man told me those things. I didn't need to know anything else, at least when I was deciding whether to meet him. I would look for the rest of the non-negotiables on the first date.

I didn't think I was any different from any other lonely single person. People have their lists. Some people don't like to *admit* that they have long lists, sometimes even to themselves. Did it make me appear petty? A friend said to me that my list may sound deep and important, but it was shallow and trivial. I argued with her and told her that trivial and shallow would be me searching for a rich man whom I could control, who was kind enough but without spiritual and emotional depth. I would ignore the fact that his job involved doing terrible things because he gave me a small bit of what I wanted. Security. Money. Why did those things matter? Trivial would be settling for a beige life.

That's shallow. I wanted a prismatic, rainbow life.

"You don't get it," she said. "Your list is so long and specific. While the things *you* seek are important to you, your list is too long and petty. You want a man who believes in spiritual and metaphysical things—and you won't settle for less? Some would say that's shallow. Unrealistic. After all, love is love, right?" She hadn't known I was dying. Maybe she would have reacted differently had she known. I ignored her words. My list would stand.

They say you don't choose whom you love. While that's partially true, and believe me, I know, I also know there are limits to that. Any wise woman would want a man who is brimming with positive attributes, someone who loves them and who they love in return. Any wise woman would choose to love the right man.

Unfortunately, we're not always wise. Sometimes we love without choice. Sometimes we love those who have nothing beautiful to offer us in return. Maybe it's part of the human condition—reaching for what is unattainable.

I know better now.

That's why I was being very selective and thorough as I chose the man I would love for the rest of my life. My intuition had been way off in the past. I was in a self-destructive pattern. I had so much healing to do back then, but I was in denial. I finally felt I was healed enough and was ready to trust my intuition again.

I thought a lot about whether to tell any of the men that I was dying. There would be no need for those who failed the test. But what if I found the perfect man? Would I have to tell him the truth? What would he do? Walk away? I certainly would. But if he loved me, it wouldn't matter. That's what I told myself. What if he didn't love me? *Wait.* The purpose of the quest was not only for me to love him, but he also must love me deeply in return. It's just supposed to be an end-of-life fling though…too much to think about. I would cross that bridge later. I was trying live in the moment without any worries. Later, later, later. No point worrying.

MY LIST

Journal Entry

He is a giver, without fear. He gives love, affection, and emotion through words and actions. Giving of himself and open communication. Gives affection openly.

Communication action taker—contact (texts, calls, etc.) Sends texts daily to say goodnight, good morning, or hello for no reason. This also means quickly replying to my texts, not waiting until the next day. Flowers, small gestures. Wildflowers, a random beautiful stone from a river.

Affection, touch, in public, at home, handholding. All without my asking. Small gestures—a stroke on the cheek, a gentle touch on my back, as he leads me through a door.

He is fearless. No fear. No walls.

He is understanding. He understands people at a deeper level than most and he understands how they operate.

He is nonjudgmental and open-minded.

He understands the importance of finding meaning in life and meaning in relationships. A philosopher.

A deep conversationalist about life, growth, and deeper meanings.

Understands the importance of learning and growth.

Openness to the mysteries of the Universe. A belief in something larger than himself and humanity.

Fun—dancing, adventure, travel. Sense of adventure, exploration, and the desire to travel. Local adventure.

He must love to dance and feel that sense of connection and freedom that comes from dance.

Laughter and humor—he must have an abundant sense of humor. He thinks I'm funny, too. Laughs in the face of sorrow. Silly, too.

Food and drink lover, cooking and eating—the experience is much more than the nourishment.

Intelligent and interesting, a bright and open conversationalist. Smart and quick, he understands politics, the world, and many unique subjects. He doesn't have to be an expert, but he must know enough.

Passionate, in love and in his pursuits, including a passion for something besides work or having passion and meaning in his work. Not just be in a job without meaning.

Kind—kind to others, always, kind to me, of course.

Trustworthy. He must be honest, even about negative things. Does not lie to cover up things that bother him, things he doesn't want to deal with.

Open physically and sexually, able to show affection. Confident in his body and his energy.

Independent. He must have his own life and pursuits, must not be too needy or demand too much of my time. Financially independent and emotionally independent, has his own friends, and part of his life is separate from mine. He respects my independence.

He has a positive outlook on life. He sees the good and the positive in even the most negative situations. No Eeyores.

Accepts people for who they are. Not judgmental. Believes in redemption.

No fear of emotions, emotionally available—stable, open.

Attractive—he absolutely must be attractive to me. That is subjective. He doesn't need to look like a model, but we must have the connection. Chemical. Connective. Energetic. I don't want normal or ordinary, either. I want quirky. Unique. Different. Unconventional, without fear of being different. Comfortable in his skin.

Romantic gestures, unexpected. Not just on Valentine's, etc.

Respects me—quickly replies to messages/calls. Does not belittle me.

He is a mountain man. He goes after what he wants—me. He pursues me without fear, with childlike abandon, and nothing stands in his way. He will move mountains to get to me.

Who is this man?

Am I unrealistic?

I'm not compromising.

Funny thing about my list—I don't think I meet those qualifications. I would fail the test.

THE PAINFUL PAST

I discovered several years ago, during the dramatic, painful, and somewhat obsessive (well, more than somewhat) breakup, that I was highly intuitive. I thought I had been right about so many things. And for a long time, that relationship consumed my thoughts and defined the future of romance for me. Everything that came afterward was doomed to failure, not because of destiny, but because I'd put him on a pedestal, high up, in a place where no man would ever again be able to stand. I'd believed he was *the one*. The only one, and he could never be replaced. Yes, it's true, every person is a unique individual. But the problem was that by believing he was the definition of a perfect man, I pushed every other man away.

I am so good at remembering. I can recall memories so clearly and easily, and they are infused with emotion. The past became part of my present. In romance, it wasn't only the love. It was also the men who rejected me. The men I had thrown away. The men I made throw me away. In my eyes, the failures. I remembered every detail of every romantic encounter. Entire conversations, every word, every gesture, every facial expression, every emotion.

The past haunted me for a long time. Very cliché. But it was true. I couldn't clear the memories. Whether or not I had loved any of the men made little difference. I still felt deep emotion. The emotions were simply a part of me.

Joy, pleasure, anger, sadness. It seemed everything was enhanced after him. Everything was deeper. More joyful. More painful.

I analyzed every detail, trying to figure out what had gone wrong. *It was not my fault.* None of it. Nonetheless, I analyzed every detail, every man. What did they do wrong? I needed to make sure I avoided those types of men next time. Or was it destiny speaking to me? *They aren't worthy.* Was I destined to be alone? I felt the past blocked me from a stable path and held me back from moving on. I was scared I would never fall in love again. When I was balanced, I was strong. But off-balance I was lost. And most of the time, back then, jumping from man to man, I was off-balance.

The past haunted me for a long time. Just like a romantic protagonist in a novel. *I'm writing these words to share my story, so that…*

Enough of that. That story should be done, and the chapter closed. He was gone. No more wallowing in self-pity. Unfortunately, there was still a part of me that felt things were incomplete. There was still something that needed to be done. But I had no idea what it was. It was clearly over, and we had both moved on. At least he had. I was still perpetually stuck.

The best stories are sometimes what happens after the end of love, the misadventures along the way to healing and wholeness. I held on tightly to healing, and yet my encounters with bizarre men and truly strange situations only made me feel worse. Everything failed, every single time I met a man I liked. It was as if the great hand of fate reached in and said, *"Nope. This is not for you."* Truly, I didn't think I had done anything wrong. I couldn't understand why everything failed. I felt cursed.

Finally, I learned that to gain something you need to give something up. But it was a long and painful road getting there.

I don't want to think about him anymore.

I was done with it all. But unfortunately, it wasn't as easy as I expected. There were always a few things to add here and there, just for emphasis. Just to show how much I had grown. Or at least I *thought* I had grown. It was all relative. Maybe I was still the same. Maybe I was still stuck. Maybe it was all an illusion. *Am I different? Did I imagine him? Am I dead? Who the hell knows!*

I needed to stop my thoughts.

The only thing I do know is I am happy. No, happiness is too contrived. I am at peace. Balanced. Free.

Damn it, yes, I am happy.

Joyful. Life is too short to be miserable. I was dying. I *had* to be happy and enjoy my last breaths.

THE ROSE

Journal Entry

Every rose has its thorns—the more beautiful the rose, the more painful the thorns. Those words followed me and became embedded in my mind, my heart, and my dreams. A message from a wise, mystical healer. The problem was, I misunderstood the meaning. I lived in illusion simply because I believed those words meant something entirely different. At that time, I thought because of my insane obsession that the rose signified him, the man I loved. And even though there had been (and would be more) pain, it was somehow worth it because the rose was so beautiful. He was the rose. Our love would bloom, our love was the rose.

The rose was right in front of me, perfectly positioned and freshly picked, laid in my path as if someone had purposefully left it there for me. I wondered if it was meant for someone else.

Why me?

Roses were rare and I had given up hope of finding one. I wanted to pick it up, but I was torn. My impulsive side kept telling me to go for it, and yet, a small, very quiet voice somewhere in my head told me to stop and take a minute. Something didn't feel right about the rose.

Coward. I'm supposed to pick it up.

It was the most beautiful rose I had ever seen. The fiery red petals were a deep flushed hue, passionate, the deepest scarlet red, almost too red to be sincere. It was tempting me, drawing me near, begging to be chosen. Yet, I still felt that something wasn't quite right. It wasn't in full bloom. An unripe rose, a baby bud. It wasn't yet time. I knew roses were rare, especially those that unexpectedly appeared out of nowhere. I resolutely chose not to be afraid. I edged closer, gingerly brushing the silky petals.

As I prepared to pluck the rose, I noted the stem was guarded with numerous thorns. I attempted to approach it from various angles, trying to avoid the thorns. Then I realized I would be pricked by those thorns no matter what I did.

Was it worth the risk to pluck the rose? There would be pain and blood. Nothing I couldn't handle. They were just thorns. At first reticent, but eventually, with clear intention, I pushed my fear of pain aside, reached down, and carefully grasped the rose by its stem.

So far, so good. No pain, no blood. I examined the rose, looking closer at the folds of skin, the wrapped edges protecting the heart underneath. Suddenly the rose bloomed fully. The scent was intoxicating, and I fell into a deep state of bliss. Now I understood the beauty of the rose and regretted not picking it up sooner.

However, just as suddenly as the bliss had encompassed me, I felt several severe pricks on my hand. Not small ones, but painful, deep wounds that pierced my skin. The pain traveled through my body and into my soul. I was desperately sad, poisoned by darkness. I dropped the rose. It was too much. Too much pain. How could something so beautiful hurt so much?

Was it worth it? I still didn't know.

We all encounter rare red roses in our lives. We sometimes ignore them when we see them, especially as we learn from past experiences. We understand that beauty can also bring us pain. We fear the rose, but at the same time, we desire the exquisiteness of the experience. The intoxicating bliss. The more beautiful an experience, the more beautiful the path we travel, the higher the risk we will experience deeper pain. Loving someone deeply sometimes comes with being hurt just as deeply.

The secret I had yet to discover way back then was that I was the rose. The beauty and passion, pain, and darkness. My passage through life. A painful road, especially because I felt things too deeply.

Would you rather wander off the beaten path to the side of the road and experience the bliss of the rose, knowing the pain that could come? Or just travel past the rose, always keeping your eyes on the future, the benign and narrow path? The safe path.

The rose is symbolic of the choices we make, the leaps of faith, that have unforeseen results. We don't know what will come next, but we must have the courage to accept the pain that may accompany the joy. The more beautiful the experience, the more painful those damn thorns are, and perhaps the more deeply they pierce our soul. Overcoming the fear of simply picking up the rose, we experience life in full bloom.

RED FLAG WARNING

here was he? He was nearly late. Better late than never. *Better early than late.*

I ordered a drink.

I hated online dating. The last time I stopped was after the strange and disastrous "situationship" that entangled me in its weird web. *This time it would be different.* But it was always the same. I had little hope.

Time after time, another ending, through no fault of mine. I believed I chose wisely. I sensed good in them. Somehow. But I was wrong every time. Was I being tested? *Universe, why do you keep testing me?* I must have more to learn. *I'm done learning. I just want to live. I'm tired of learning.* I felt the Universe was deceiving me, ostensibly bringing me beautiful souls, when in fact those souls were so damaged that they could hardly take care of their own lives, much less be in a healthy relationship. Liars, deceivers, and manipulators. Players. While I opened my heart and spoke my truth, they used that same truth to deceive me.

I always knew the truth. I could sense all the lies. I knew when they'd lost interest. I'm a human lie detector. It was intuitive. Psychic. *I wish I could sense it before I got involved in anything.* Prevent anything bad from happening. *Why can't I see through them when I first meet them?* Something clouded my judgment on that first date.

Hopefulness? Desperation?

Maybe they had good intentions in the beginning. Maybe we all do. But then something goes wrong. Maybe the more things progressed, the more the screwed-up parts of them came out. *It wasn't me.* I was balanced and open. They were unstable and closed. Even if I had intuitive *pings*, warning signs, which I did, I kept moving forward, trying to make things work. *Why did I ignore it all?*

I questioned my decision to get back into dating. Is this really how I wanted to spend my last months? On a quest for a perfect man? At least I had my intuition to guide me. I would use it this time. I had honed it well—nothing would escape detection. I wouldn't ignore red flags anymore.

As I waited for my date to arrive, I decided to be merciless. There is no perfection without trial. This would be his trial. Would he be the perfect man, the man worthy of my time? I was early and he was not. I waited patiently, my mind flowing to the past and the last man I'd dated before my current celibacy, the one who I thought finally knocked some sense into me.

PLAYING POKER WITH THE QUEEN OF HEARTS

Journal Entry

I couldn't see my cards. Everything was blurry. I held them in my hand and looked over to my right. The Queen of Hearts sat there, hiding her cards. She was hidden in the shadows, and I couldn't see her clearly. There was a dense fog surrounding everything. I didn't know what to do next. I was nervous. I held the cards tightly, gripping them until they bent. I wasn't going to let her see. But could she? I still didn't know what I held in my hand. Did it even matter? I took a risk and laid my cards on the table.

The fog was gradually lifting, and I could see the Queen had her back to me. She sat perfectly still. Then she slowly turned her head toward me. That's when I saw my face. It was me, but I was different. I looked more confident and fearless. An assertive, ruthless Queen. She stared at my cards. She smiled. Then she laid down her hand. Five aces. *Impossible*. There was an ace I hadn't seen before. It was an infinity symbol. The ace of infinity. Fate, destiny, divine intervention. She gathered all the cards from the table, put them in her pocket, and walked away. I knew she had taken something from me, and I wanted it back.

I got up to follow her, but I couldn't move. I struggled to pick up my feet and move in her direction, but I could not. The only path I could take was in the opposite direction, out the door. I walked away, through the only exit I could see. I knew then I had no control. My fate was out of my hands. She had walked away with my freedom of choice, my free will.

It was just a dream, but that's how I felt. As if I had no control over my emotions. As if they weren't my own. I would be happy one minute, and the next, a thought or idea would pop into my head, and I would be sobbing. It didn't feel right. It wasn't me. I wondered if I was depressed. But I didn't feel depressed. I experienced only moments of chaos. There was anarchy in my heart. Part of me had mutinied and followed the Queen.

This was what remained after gambling for love. I'd made so many mistakes. Playing my cards without knowing what they were. Not knowing about the hidden ace. Not knowing that the Queen of Hearts always wins. Maybe I wasn't supposed to know. I was supposed to gamble and take the risk. But why? Yes, many lessons had been learned. But I wanted to know why. Why did I need to learn them? Why had I been chosen? Is life just a game? Do we play with or against ourselves, our souls, or the Universe? And who wins? I didn't. I felt lost. And all I wanted to know was—why? In the grand scheme of life, a broken heart is small. There are bigger sorrows. But then why had this pain felt so deep? Maybe if had been able to see the cards, I would have understood.

I couldn't control my thoughts or actions. I believed what I believed. I thought I'd seen all the cards. I'd been given glimpses as they were shuffled and dealt. I'd been so sure the cards were a winning hand. Yet, I was afraid. Deep down, I probably knew the truth but refused to accept it.

When I finally picked the cards up, it was too late. I was already all in. The glimpses of the signs and messages on their own showed a beautiful outcome. Love. Love was the answer, and love was enough to change the outcome. Read together, they told a different story. They'd led me down a path of illusion. I was alone with this hand, and I was the only one who loved. He didn't love me, at least not in the same way, and he had already finished the game. He'd folded a long time ago, not daring to challenge the Queen the Hearts. He was a lot smarter than I was.

Hope and faith had blinded me, and desire had clouded my heart and had overtaken my mind—the desire for something that had never been mine and never would be. What a fool I had been. So many wasted years. Although it was my fault for misinterpreting everything, I still couldn't get past the fact that the Universe had guided me down that path. To what end? I had no idea, except perhaps the harsh lessons would somehow help me on my journey. What was the point? I felt old, and time was speeding by too quickly. What was the point of lessons so late in life? Was my search for love over? Would I be alone now for the rest of my life? Was my purpose to find the answers in solitude? I felt so alone. Nobody understood. I was tired. Life had exhausted me.

In a few short years, life had given me a larger burden than all the years before. I felt as if I had lived many lives, each more difficult than the one before, and I didn't want to return after my death. If I died right now, I would choose not to reincarnate again. I was done. Being human is exhausting, like carrying a heavily weighted sack, without even knowing what's inside. I leave the burdens of this life in the past, and I move forward. I can't carry them anymore.

LAST MAN OUT

The last man I'd dated post-heartbreak, was shortly before my diagnosis. I didn't have any hope or expectations, but it was doomed from the start. In this rarity of moments, I knew right from the beginning that it was never going to work. As soon as I met him, on our very first date, I thought to myself, *He isn't right for me.* It wasn't anything he did or said. It was just a knowing. But still, I moved forward. *Why?* I decided that instead of making quick judgments, I should be more patient and move slowly, flowing with things. Plus, at that point, I didn't trust my intuition. I had created too many messes and blamed them on my inability to read things clearly.

Before meeting him, I was already frustrated with dating. I'd taken a short sabbatical. Only two months, but to me, that was a long time. I discovered I was happier single. I found my inner peace without a man. I wondered, *Why had I jumped back in?* I was happy. Why mess with happiness? I thought about it for a long time—whether I was ready or if I even wanted to date. But I felt bold and confident. Nothing could throw me off, and I was in full control. I would date, maybe have a fling or two. Nothing serious. Who knew what would happen? Maybe the man of my dreams was just within my reach. And if not, at least I would have fun.

I glided into my date with coolness. No fear. I was completely in control.

Three months later, it was done—via email. You know, the way spineless people break up with you when they're afraid to speak the truth to your face. I laughed when I read his email. I did. I laughed out loud. Although I knew it was coming, I was surprised by his method. I hadn't seen him as the type of person who would avoid confrontation. Then I realized, *that when you lie, it makes it much harder to speak in person.* And because of all his lies, he couldn't speak to me directly. He had to email. It made it easier for him. I didn't want to let him off the hook so easily, though. I ignored the email, pretending I never received it.

Buried in the email were the lies I already knew. I had sensed the deception in my intuition much earlier. However, for some reason, I had let it all go. I guess I wanted to see what would happen. Maybe I was testing him to see if he would eventually tell me the truth. Instead, he told more lies. I should've been angrier and more hurt, but I wasn't. Maybe just my pride was hurt, a little.

How dare he reject me? I should have rejected him after all his lies. I'd already known what was happening and that he planned to break up with me.

After a few days, he called me. I ignored him. What was the point? It was over. However, part of me wanted to answer so I could verify the lies, sense them in his voice. It seemed so easy for him to lie, at least on the outside. I didn't sense guilt, but maybe he was an expert at hiding his feelings. I wanted validation, to prove to myself I was right. *I hate being right.* I just ignored him and let it go. He texted and tried to call a few more times, but I never answered. He wasn't worth the effort.

I didn't understand why I'd put myself through all of it. From the beginning, I knew it wasn't going to work. I knew about the deception, and I waited. It became a game of chicken. Who would speak first? He must have known that I knew. I think people are a lot more intuitive than I sometimes give them credit for—even the dumb deceivers. Deep down, we always know the truth.

He was handsome. *No, he was hot.* He was extremely hot. He appeared kind, and he was funny. He made me laugh, and any laughter was good. He was also deeply passionate about me. He couldn't keep his hands off me. He would call me in the middle of the night and beg me to come over. I felt the same way about him and easily got in my car and slipped into his bed at two a.m. Were these some of the red flags I chose to ignore? *Who does those crazy, impulsive things?*

At first, it was just a sense that something was off, that he was not who he seemed, that he was hiding something. However, I was determined to be with him, even with the subtle red flags. I was having fun, and I didn't feel any emotional entanglement, so I was certain there would be no heartbreak. I talked myself into it. I had taken life too seriously in the past, and it was time for something different. I was all in, despite the red flags waving right in front of my face.

Unfortunately, my emotions got in the way. I started having feelings for him. I tried not to. I tried to keep it light and distant. I knew he only wanted a fling, that he wasn't serious about me. He didn't even need to speak the words— casual, no strings attached, no commitment. We spent a lot of time together, mostly in bed. And eating. That's all we did, eat and fuck. I tried to deny the feelings of love—no, not love—lust? Attachment? I was happy, and I didn't want my feelings to get in the way. I didn't want things to end. So I disregarded the warnings, blaming them on my fear of abandonment.

It's just your fear, ignore it.

And so I did, despite the nagging sensation of wrongness deep down in my gut.

Maybe happiness is more important than love. And I was happy.

Until I wasn't. I was right. There were many hidden things I didn't know about. He was a high-functioning addict. Alcohol, drugs, probably sex. I should have seen that clearly. But more importantly, he was also sleeping with other people. Many people. We never talked about being exclusive, but still, you'd think someone would have enough respect to tell you the truth, especially when you asked them point blank—*Are you dating other people?* And I had asked him. Twice, at least. I wanted to know.

He denied it at the beginning. He denied it in the middle. And he denied it in the end. Many lies. Not only about who he slept with, but about who he was. From the very beginning, I knew something was wrong, but instead of calling him out, I stayed quiet. I felt my intuition was telling me to wait.

Wait for what?

I already knew the truth. Was my intuition wrong? Staying with him made little sense to me. In my head, I told myself there was a lesson to learn. I needed to be patient. In the past, I'd always acted impulsively, ending things and walking away. This time, I decided to wait and see what would happen. Right or wrong, at that moment I thought that was my best course of action.

I waited for him to act, and nothing happened. Everything stayed the same, stagnant, and at the same time, confusing. When I first sensed his indifference, I decided to stop communicating with him.

A test, a game.

His texts and phone calls grew further apart. Banal texts, empty of anything except formal politeness. I forced myself to send short replies, then I finally decided it was time to move on. I knew I should officially end things, but I refused to break up with him. I wanted him to have the courage to say the words. That's why, when he finally emailed me, I wasn't shocked.

He was a coward. Just like all the others.

All I wanted was for him to be honest, to speak the truth. Redeem himself. What did it matter? Why should I be worried about his redemption? I did what I did at the time for reasons still unknown.

I hate liars. I'd rather hear painful truths than beautiful lies.

I wished I had seen the details, but the only thing my intuition told me was that something was wrong. I couldn't see the details. *I only saw what I wanted to see.* Only the good. My problem was my expectations and visions clouded reality. I expected him to be a certain way when clearly, he wasn't. I expected I'd be able to keep my feelings out of the relationship, but clearly, I couldn't. *I'm too loyal.* One man at a time. It was a terrible mistake. I had falsely presumed he wasn't sure about me. Or he was fearful. Or he was healing from a messy breakup. *Or he was just stupid.* I formulated lots of excuses. But never the real answer—that he'd deceived and manipulated me. I had been easy prey.

WEAKEST LINK

Why do people do these things? Cheating, lying, and sleeping with several people at once. *Maybe I'm a prude.* I knew many who casually dated and slept around, and it didn't faze them at all. I didn't judge them. It was the opposite. I wished I could be like them. *I am an emotional weakling.* It was all disaster after disaster because my emotions got in the way. *No. It was their fault. The men I meet are the ones who are screwed up.*

In a moment of weakness, I once told another man that I thought I loved him. I didn't say I did. Only that I thought I did. What did I really feel? Who knows. It was one of those impulsive things you regret as soon as the words pass over your lips. I knew he didn't love me. He was selfish and sometimes disappeared for days.

When I spoke the words, he was silent. I felt his body tense. Nothing, no words. He didn't speak a single word. I knew I had made a mistake. But I couldn't take it back. I lay there, wondering if I should say anything else. *I'm just joking.* I doubt he would have believed that. When I finally heard his deep breaths, I realized he had fallen asleep. Nothing else to be done. I knew what was coming.

I woke up the next morning and he was gone, leaving without saying goodbye. We never saw each other again. It was over as soon as I uttered the words. I didn't realize until later that I didn't love him. Why did I say it then? Maybe I was just too desperate to keep him around. Maybe I thought that by expressing my love, I would make things better. It didn't make any sense. I knew the situation, and I knew it was pointless. Maybe I'd just been caught up in a passionate moment. Whatever my reasons, I was hurt by his sudden departure. And I was angry at myself for being desperate, for wanting to stay with someone who could never give me what I wanted in return.

Cheaters. Evading exposure. I didn't love them, yet I wanted them to stay. I didn't want to be rejected. Even though they were jerks. I swore I wasn't hurt by their rejections. I had already accepted many things for what they were. And I had already released many of them by the time they broke up with me. But it did hurt and triggered some deep emotions and my fear of abandonment. On the surface, it was a fleeting pain. But on a deeper level, the feelings were pronounced, like PTSD.

By that point, I assumed my intuition was off when it came to men. I didn't trust myself. But the truth was my intuition had always been on point. I just chose to ignore the signs and warnings. I ignored the red flags, the nagging feelings, the jolts to the gut. I realized I was ignoring my intuition because of a larger fear—the fear of being alone for the rest of my life. *I am old.* I was losing my physical appearance, my charm. This was my power. I used my looks to get what I wanted. A lot. I knew how to smile. I knew what men wanted. I could be anything they wanted me to be. A chameleon. I was a complete fake.

THE BUS

Journal Entry

I met him in a square. He was waiting for a bus. Even though I didn't know where he was going, I decided to go with him. He didn't invite me, but he said, "Okay," when I told him. I packed all my belongings on the bus. A green bus. He showed me a piece of art he'd painted. It was rolled up, a beautiful piece that included every color imaginable. A rainbow. He handed it to me just as I was suddenly called home. I had to go turn off all the lights. It took forever, because I got sidetracked by a woman wearing a fur coat. She needed help sorting clothes. Very strange. By the time I got back, both he and the bus were gone. All my possessions were gone. What did he take with him? My heart? My soul?

I had a second dream about the green bus. I was riding the bus, going through a traffic circle. As the bus started around the circle, I saw him sitting in the center, in the lotus pose. I banged on the window, trying to get his attention. He needed to get on! But he didn't move. The bus kept going, and I watched him as he was left behind.

We were never in sync, and we were always on buses going in different directions. Moving to new places, always alone. That was the perfect metaphor for our relationship.

WE ARE ALL BROKEN

Why am I doing this? I thought about texting my date and canceling. He was, after all, only the first one on my quest. There would be others. *I'm too early. Do I care more than he does?* My mind had gone into overdrive, delving into the past and analyzing my past mistakes. *Maybe I shouldn't be dating.* He wasn't even there yet and already I was worrying and overthinking. I had wished he would just arrive so I could get it over with. Then I remembered why I was meeting him. I had to find the perfect man.

Things were simpler when I was younger. I somehow made all the right choices when it came to relationships. I didn't think about my words or actions. I was just living in the moment. My mind was clear. There were no arguments with my heart. I was also always treated with respect and kindness. Breakups happened in person, and people weren't afraid. I was never so deeply wounded that I couldn't bounce back from the pain.

But was it real? Or had I been asleep?

Now…it seems men are screwed up. People are screwed up. People my age are broken. Bitter from painful divorces and heartbreak. People who had invested many years of their lives in marriages that fell apart. Kids. Money. Things were simpler when I was younger.

But these men. They were all a mess. They were all screwed up. I was normal. I'd suffered pain and my own personal tragedies, but I had come out on top and strong. The others, the ones who seemed broken, were weak. They were not self-aware and couldn't see their brokenness. Maybe I was blind. I just didn't have the clarity and understanding to see their pain, and that they too were afraid. I didn't see that others had also suffered pain and that everyone was healing. I had entered relationships as a martyr, the survivor of a broken heart, thinking they should have understood me and offered me love and healing.

Everyone is just as broken as I am. How they react after those midlife breakups defines how they move forward. And sometimes, in moving forward, they make mistakes. Just like me. But back then, their mistakes were weaknesses in my eyes. *I am the only one who can make mistakes because of my pain.* I was angry. I knew those men had issues. I knew there were complications in their lives. But I refused to accept that they were broken too. I simply walked away or forced them to walk away.

It was all their fault. I was healing, I told myself. They should have treated me better. I imagined I was the only one suffering. I didn't acknowledge their suffering until much later. Back then, they were malevolent. And I was a saint.

TRUTH

Journal Entry

What is truth? Is anything true? I mean, I once thought some things were true. Even about myself. I wove myself into a character I believed was beautiful and full of love and light. Then I lost faith in myself and the magic of the Universe. The character changed. She became pain and darkness. All I wanted was to be love and light, but I was afraid my heart would deceive me again. I focused on logic. He wasn't there. He'd walked away. He was gone. Why would anyone in their right mind wait? So many sad, broken people waiting for lost loves. Twin flames. Soulmates. They all believed they were destined to be together, just as I did at one time. At what point did I get totally lost and become like those sad souls?

Twin flames were just an excuse, something people tell themselves when they're afraid to let go because of the pain. They believe in a magical connection, holding on for dear life, so they don't have to face the truth and the pain. They fail to see that they have free will, that they can walk away. Perhaps their connection was simply a learning experience—a soul contract, a karmic lesson.

I don't believe in twin flames anymore. All over the internet, it was a money-making business that seemed to take advantage of people who were broken and in pain.

These twin flame "coaches" took your money and promised you that if you did certain things, your runaway twin flame would return. Even the free advice was similar. Heal, follow your path, and your twin will return. The trick was both of you needed to heal. So there were no guarantees. I once believed that if I healed, he would return. On the surface, healing is a beautiful and necessary concept. But healing for the sake of being reunited with someone was an illusion. Was your purpose truly to connect with another person so you could achieve ultimate happiness? I don't believe that. *Happiness comes from within.* Or so I tell myself.

I do believe in soulmates. But they aren't always for the rest of your life. They sometimes come and go, each time leaving an imprint, teaching lessons, and expanding your spiritual growth. Most importantly, they aren't always romantic.

Romance is a product of society. Movies, books, and music infiltrate our minds and hearts, convincing us to believe romantic love is the highest form of love. Everyone wants their happily ever after without realizing it's just a construct created by the disconnection in our society. Love and connections are everywhere, but we deny ourselves the opportunities to connect and love in a non-romantic way. I don't know why. It's a deep question. The importance of romantic love—maybe it's all about procreation. Maybe it's a physical expression of what we feel but are unable to express at a higher, energetic level. We are human. Most of us are lost and are unable to connect at a deeper level. The individual, the ego, searches for romantic love to fill the void in our souls and find the truth behind our existence and purpose.

I searched for truth everywhere, but then when the truth was too painful, I stopped. Everything became a lie. I lost my faith. And that's when I made mistakes. I think I needed to make those mistakes because maybe it would eventually bring me back to faith. Not faith in romantic love. The search for truth is the search for self-love. I hoped so.

BACK TO REALITY

I still had a few more minutes until he arrived. I was way too early, as usual. *I should leave and then come back a few minutes late.* Someone once told me to always arrive for a date five minutes late and make a grand entrance. I wasn't a very good game player, though. I was trying to live with honesty and authenticity. That's probably why I had so many problems. I certainly hoped I had made the right decision to search for a perfect man. Was this the best way to spend the rest of my short life?

I hadn't given too much thought to my death. My mind may be wild with random thoughts, but one thing was true. The most terrible things were rarely what was on my mind. I spent hours dissecting and ruminating about whether I had made the right decisions in love and very little time thinking about my death. I was completely fine with it. Most people would be in an existential frenzy. But I was already there and had been there for a long time, so it easily became part of my reality. Just like my daily cup of coffee, it was intertwined with my routine, a normal part of my day that didn't require any thought.

Let's see, do I have time to do this before I die? My primary focus was finding a perfect man.

I always spoke my truth. I was very clear from the beginning of any relationship how much I valued honesty. And yet, there were lies. I also told them I was very good at reading people. I guess they didn't believe that, either. I get it—they probably didn't want to tell me the truth, to admit what they had done wrong. Just like many others. One even said he'd like to be friends. *My friends don't lie to me.* I said *sure*, knowing I would never want to be his friend. I just wanted to let things go without too much drama. *Goodbye. Good riddance.*

In the past, what started as hope—the possibilities and potentials in swiping seeming endless—slowly moved toward cynicism and frustration. I gradually affirmed my decision to cut back on dating and eventually stopped dating entirely. At least for a short time. Was I making mistakes, or did I choose wrongly? Or did the Universe have other plans for me? Was it a matter of fate or free will? I had no damned idea. Only that I had become sick and tired of feeling like a pawn in a game.

I knew my biggest mistake was hoping I could potentially love them—and that they could love me. I was searching for love, and I felt love was consistently taken away. *It wasn't meant to be*, I told myself. The Universe had intervened and made it go away. It's much easier and less painful to say that a man was not for me. *The Universe had stepped in and made him a cheating liar because I wasn't supposed to be with him.* Looking back, my thoughts made zero sense. The belief that the Universe, God, was saving me released me from my own responsibility. It also released the other person of responsibility. *It was meant to happen. Not his fault. Not mine, either.*

I do believe in divine intervention, but why would the Universe act in such trivial circumstances? It's not as if death was involved, or some significant tragedy. Divine intervention should be saved for truly meaningful things.

Not for a small, personal misfortune that was perhaps just an injury to my pride. I knew in the end that I didn't love any of those men. I was just caught up in the moment. It was both comforting and ego-pleasing, and I relished the attention. Fun times, not meant to last, whether by fate or circumstance. I moved on quickly.

SITTING IN SILENCE

He was late. It was now 7:05 p.m. and I was irritated. Should I text him?

Be patient, I told myself. I decided to wait five more minutes.

He walked in at 7:30. I should have left at 7:10. I was annoyed—at him for being late, and at myself for waiting.

He waved and walked over.

Not even an apology. I could already sense his arrogance. He was handsome. Hot. He probably thought he could get any woman he wanted.

I should've said something. Spoken up.

When did I stop speaking up for myself? I used to be annoyingly vocal about my needs. I spoke what was on my mind. No filter. Many times, this wasn't a great thing, but at least I spoke up and let things out. It was too much. Too much truth and people couldn't handle it. It sometimes created an imbalance in relationships when the dark truth came out. People rarely wanted to face the truth.

Whatever it was, I decided to keep quiet. In the recent past, if a man had decided not to call me for several days, he was gone. No more wasted time. In the more distant past, I would have let it go out of desperation. Now, I found myself letting it all go again. Nothing bothered me except the fact that nothing bothered me. I should be upset. I should yell, scream, complain, or at least talk about it. What was wrong with me? I was a woman of extremes, who either spoke too much or said nothing at all.

Only later did I realize that there were many times I should have spoken up. I thought my intuition was telling me to flow. I'd misinterpreted that. Flowing is great, but it doesn't mean you let yourself be treated like shit. Because things did bother me more than I admitted, and not just with this late date. But I was determined to flow. I forced myself. But I wasn't flowing. And I realized I told men many half-truths—about myself, about what I wanted. So, in my own way, I was a liar. I was a self-editor. I would only say what was strategically beneficial. I was constantly preparing the *right* words to say.

I didn't say a word to my date. I wanted to leave, but I just sat and waited for him to say something. I quickly went through various possible conversations in my head. None of them were pleasant. I decided to stay silent.

SELF-EDITING

Journal Entry

A man once told me I self-edit a lot.

I thought about it for a few seconds and realized I knew exactly what he meant. Thoughts and words. Actions too. I thought through things before I initiated some sort of action or spoke any words.

I pretended to be confused by his words, but I knew—I always wanted to say the right thing and take the right action. Did I even understand what was right or wrong? I was trying to accomplish something with the redlining of my life, but I wasn't sure what. Past perfectionism, perhaps. Or fear of future failure.

"What do you mean?" I asked, a falsely puzzled look on my face.

I pretended to be baffled, but he could read me better than I expected. Nobody had ever been able to read me so clearly, to see right through the façade I presented to the world. That bothered me immensely. I was an actress on a stage playing the part I felt they wanted me to play. Like the chameleon, I wanted to adapt to what they wanted to see. I could be anything, and I believed that enabled me to get anything. I could play the part of the worldly seductress or the naïve innocent. Whatever they wanted, I found it easy to acquiesce. The malleable chameleon. For me, it was a challenge to see if I could be everything they wanted. And hopefully, I would get everything I wanted in return.

He laughed.

"Come on. You know what I mean. Don't play the innocent."

I hesitated and then flashed my mesmerizing, seductive smile.

I will draw you in, and you will forget the what and the why.

"That won't work with me," he said as he took my hand.

I felt a strange but recognizable vibration as I casually slid my hand out of his grasp. I wanted no more of those energetic vibes.

"You're so funny. I know who I am, and I don't pretend to be something I'm not," I told him, hoping he would believe the words that I hardly believed myself.

I kissed him, to make him forget. He kissed me back, and there it was, that energetic sexual connection, the magic eraser of unwanted questions. As I kissed him deeper, I knew I had him in my power. No more questions. I controlled everything. I wrapped my arms around him, pulling in closer. I could almost feel myself passing through him.

When he touched me, I tried to stay in control. I tried to keep seducing him, but with his touch, he intuitively understood what to do. It was an instant pleasure. He knew me. I was lost. I have little memory of the actions, only the exquisite, endless pleasure.

I draped my leg over him, wanting to be as close as possible to him.

"That was amazing," I whispered in his ear.

His hand swept down the length of my body, his feathery light fingertips giving me goosebumps. I felt a sudden chill. He pulled me closer.

"You want more?" he whispered back.

It was like this the whole night. I don't know how long. I lost all sense of time with him. Was this love? I wanted love, but I wasn't sure—is sex love? Is love sex? They were intertwined in my mind. I couldn't separate the two. That upset me. I wish I could be free to not get attached. I couldn't. They were inseparable. Once I felt him, I wanted him more. It was trouble, I knew. Because most people didn't think the way I did. They just wanted the outside part, the physical, the body. To them, it was separate. Sex and love were opposites and to have both was rare. I felt there was something wrong with me, but at the same time, I was upset that they were unable to see me—the real me. They just saw the skin of the goddess without seeing her soul.

But he claimed to see me. The me who wasn't me. If he could see through the fake me, and then see the real me, what exactly did he see? What did it mean? Did he love me? I fell instantly in love with him at that moment, and I desperately hoped he loved me. I was happy and simultaneously lonely. Separated from myself. I knew it would end badly. I knew he would leave. He just wanted the goddess. The statue. Not the heart. I knew that. Yet I held on tighter.

It didn't end well. It was no surprise to me.

THE PARADOX OF
PAIN AND FEAR

I didn't want to mess things up. I didn't want to reveal too much about myself, my weaknesses and my fears. My imperfections. I kept the deep parts hidden, but always smiling, always pretending everything was okay on the outside. Why was it so important to show that I was fine, that nothing fazed me or hurt me? Pride? Or just the simple fact that I didn't want people to know they'd affected me in some way, therefore giving them power over me? And how would they have power over me, and what would it matter? *They can't hurt me if they don't know my weaknesses.* I was protecting myself. *No more pain,* I said. Everything would be on my terms. Everything would flow the way I wanted it to. I would control everything.

It sounded easy in theory. The fear of pain is a lot more complex. Our fears are intertwined at a far deeper level than we realize. All fears come from the fear of pain. It's so hard to grasp how they work together when we are constantly trying to avoid pain. Instead of fusing these together, we pull them apart, causing us to separate the pain and fear until they are unrecognizable. Society constantly tells us to be strong, and that being fearful is an act of cowardice. *Just fight it, be strong, and don't be a wimp.* We are discouraged from asking for help. If you don't fight fear and push away your pain, you are weak.

The reality is it takes a lot more courage to face our fears. When someone tells us to just stop being afraid, they are telling us to ignore the fear—repress it, and it will go away. It's unlikely that will happen, especially those very deep fears of which we're even not aware. I jumped right into many new relationships even when I was fearful of being rejected and hurt. I ended up sabotaging many connections because of fear. *I didn't even know.*

I let the lies flow past. I should have said something about the lies. Called out that last man. But I chose not to.

And I chose to accept the lateness of my current date.

Everything does happen for a reason, whether it's to learn from or whether it's not meant to be doesn't matter in the end, as long as we understand and grow from the experience. Wise advice. But wise advice is rarely followed.

And what, exactly, am I learning? I asked myself, as my date, Alan, sat down and proceeded to order food and drinks for me without asking what I wanted.

LIFE IS A HARSH LESSON

What is the purpose of life? What is the meaning behind the everyday existence we lead? Why is it such a struggle? The purpose of life is love. We struggle because we lose sight of what it means to love. If we're out of balance, we strive for material gain and power. We build relationships based on the desire for security instead of love. We let others define our meaning. We let others control our happiness. We are out of balance.

We are here to learn how to love. Sometimes these are hard lessons, sometimes small understandings. But mostly hard. From the day we are born until the day we pass into the light, there is no end to learning. But I wish there was. I'm tired of learning. I know looking at life and experiences as one gigantic lesson will give me peace. There is no such thing as good or bad luck, and we do have control over our lives. If we look at the negative not as another terrible thing that happened but as an opportunity for growth, we release some of the pain. We reclaim the power we have over our feelings.

This requires us to look back. But anything, in retrospect, is always better. When living in the very moment of difficult experiences, it's impossible to see the life lesson in which we are entangled. That's the point about lessons. This is not an "a-ha" statement. We all know this. Yet we don't. In moments of pain and challenge, we forget.

I think if we can stop ourselves in those moments and try to understand why we're being challenged, we can stop dwelling on the negativity. What do I have to learn? Why do I keep repeating these same cycles, those same behaviors, and ultimately reliving the same types of relationships? Why?

I know why…but I can't stop. *I've learned my damned lesson.* And yet, I'm still repeating the same scenarios over and over. I just keep choosing the wrong ones. They are as broken as me, and two broken people together don't stand a chance. All I'm doing is creating a toxic codependent relationship full of unhappiness that ultimately affects my self-worth and lowers my self-esteem, and most importantly, causes me to lose hope and give up. *Phew.* Relationship Psychology 101 in a nutshell.

Learn your lesson. *I did!* If I keep repeating these patterns without learning, I will stay stuck. *I stopped!* I keep choosing these people, so, clearly, I haven't learned.

Fuck dating.

MOVING FORWARD

I don't want to write about the past anymore. The lost opportunities. Especially the one significant lost chance, the one that changed my life. But it keeps coming back as if the story is not complete. What more needs to be written? Nothing. Everything. I know that's not true. It's done. I keep revisiting things, though, because I feel it's necessary for healing and growth. At least that's what I tell myself. I don't dwell on the past, and I try not to regret it, but I know I need to examine the things I've lived through to heal and grow. And every experience, be it now or in the future, is affected by the past. It's important to examine ourselves and our experiences to see where we went wrong and to make sure we stop making the same mistakes over and over again. I repeated those mistakes for far too long until I finally realized that the "stuckness" in my life was not because of others but because of myself and my failure to learn what I needed to learn.

This was not exactly new. I had known this for a long time. I just needed to put it into practice. It was hard.

WHO IS THIS MAN?

I let Alan order. I let it go. It wasn't that important to me. Our drinks arrived, and he immediately peppered me with questions.

"So how are you? How was your day? What exciting thing happened to you today?" he asked as he downed his scotch. A double.

I slowly reached for my drink, took a dainty sip, and smiled.

"Just a regular day. A good day, but quiet," I replied.

I was trying to figure him out, to read him, to determine what he wanted from me. Searching for the best answers to his questions.

There was no stopping him.

"What was good?"

"And why quiet?"

"Do you like quiet?"

"What's a regular day?"

Too many questions. I didn't even know what to say. I was usually the one asking questions. I was taken aback.

Before I could answer, he stated, "Oh, I got tickets for a little blues club nearby. In about an hour and a half. We have time to eat."

He didn't ask me. He'd decided for me—again. All within fifteen minutes of meeting me. And he was late. I was annoyed.

"Sorry, I can't do that. You should have asked me first. I need to get back home for an online class I'm taking," I lied, hoping he'd believe me.

I glanced at my phone.

"I only have about an hour," I continued.

Another lie.

"Okay," he replied, staring at me with a puzzled look, "then you will have to be quick and answer my questions."

Really? I continued to smile—a stiffly suspended smile. *Get it over with.*

"Number one: today was good because nothing bad happened. Number two: it was quiet because there was nobody around asking incessant questions. Number three: yes, I love peace and quiet. And, finally, number four: a regular day is a day of peace and quiet."

"Okay, then. How about this? Why are you here still? What annoys you most? Do you think you can control people?" he asked.

He was relentless.

"Why are you asking me all these questions?" I asked, "Can we just have a conversation, a normal back-and-forth conversation?"

He smirked—an annoying smirk that pretended to know more than he let on.

"Why are you still here?" he asked as he gulped a full glass of scotch. I didn't even see him order it.

I should have known this would prove to be just another annoying date. *Why hadn't I learned*? Dating is over for me. I'm doomed to be alone for the rest of my forever.

I didn't want to answer him. I wanted to get up and go. But I forced myself to reply, just to get him to leave me alone. *I will speak, then leave.*

"Because I'm too nice," I replied as I stood up.

He rose and lightly touched my shoulder.

"Stop, please. I'm really sorry. I don't mean to play games. I'm not that person. It's just been a long time since I've dated. I have no idea what I'm doing,"

He appeared honest and earnest in his reply. I wanted to believe him, but I was done believing in dating and love and other impossible things. If he was nervous, he was very good at hiding it. I hadn't sensed anything except arrogance.

I wanted a new beginning, but this was all wrong.

"I'm sorry, I can't do this," I said.

I walked out as quickly as I could and ran to my car, hoping he wasn't following me.

He wasn't.

Time for something new, better than men, better than love. Better than this! I put off my search for the perfect man.

I AM THE CENTER OF THE UNIVERSE

I would focus on myself and what I wanted to do. No more wasted energy. I didn't have time for that. I could make my own choices without being encumbered by desire and connection to a man. If I wanted to pack up and go somewhere for a week, I could. If I wanted to stay home for a week and eat junk food, I could. I had burdened myself by attaching myself to those who weren't right for me. It wasn't healthy. It was wrong.

Universe, thank you for intervening and saving me from disaster. It was time for a bigger change, a new adventure without men.

THE QUEST

tarting on a new adventure sounds exciting. Tantalizing. Something fresh and different. A walk into the unknown. A walk on the wild side? Maybe… that depends. All I knew was that I felt the pull to explore. A cross-country trip. Lots of driving. Staying in unknown places. By myself. It didn't feel very exciting when I first thought about it. Adventure seemed more adventurous in another country. My intuition was telling me, *I must go.* There was something I needed to find.

True love?

Ha. That would be a miracle, and I wasn't sure I believed in miracles anymore. I wasn't searching for love anymore. I was focusing on myself and staying away from the complications of relationships. Plus, I was dying. No point in getting entangled with anyone. That would have to wait until the afterlife. Or a future lifetime.

I had no idea what I was searching for—I was on a mysterious quest without answers. All those puzzles in my journals from many years ago were still unsolved. All the synchronistic events that took place, all the insane and amazing people I connected with over time. I dutifully wrote everything down. *My journal must have all the answers.* On every page I turned, the answer was love. *Love is the answer* was a trite, contrived response. Was that part of the quest or part of my unbalanced and obsessive mind?

And love—was it romantic or self-love or love of humanity? *Which was more important?* And around and around went my thoughts, bouncing from journal page to journal page until I was even farther from the truth.

I realized my problem. I had too many answers, but I had no idea what the question was. If love was the answer, I couldn't do much unless I knew the question. The answer to what? *Life? Happiness? Enlightenment?* I was confused. The answers were meaningless, drifting alone. Perhaps this was a journey for the QUESTions. Maybe that had been my problem all along—not knowing what to ask. Somehow, being on my own, traveling through the country during a pandemic, I would discover the answers. I didn't believe that completely, but I was bored and frustrated and ready to go.

NEW BEGINNINGS

I quickly closed the window and flipped the lock. I walked through each room, checking for forgotten items and assessing the emotions I felt, the memories of my short but meaningful time in the house. My home. Just a few years—a short time in the many years of my life, but a significant time. Empty rooms. In my office, the clutter was gone. I slowly made my way downstairs. I closed my eyes and envisioned the gatherings, the laughter, and the chaos. Memories. Nostalgia. My hand touched the wall, and I felt the small cracks in the paint, slowly gliding my hand along the wall until it abruptly stopped, and my hand floated in the air. *The end.* I made my way toward the back door. It still looked the same. *Nothing has changed. Yet?* I opened the sliding glass door and sat down on the stairs of the back deck. My solace. My countless hours here, even on frigid winter days. Watching birds, writing, drinking my morning coffee, and feeling the warm sun on my face. I closed my eyes. *I will miss this temporary home far more than I had expected.* It had been the witness to so many things. As they say, if these walls could spill their secrets…or maybe they would say something else entirely.

Buzz. My phone vibrated. I was jerked back to reality. It was my friend, asking me if I was on my way yet.

I stood up and quickly looked around one last time, taking in the green of the grass, the old, collapsing but still lovely barns, just breathing in the scent. Every place has its scent. *I will always remember this smell. I want to remember the familiar.*

I carried the last box to my car, a few random items scattered in several corners of the house. That's how I felt. Scattered and random. Nowhere definitive to go with only a few possessions. The rest was in storage. I expected this to be a monumental moment where I suddenly became free from everything in my past. As if moving out and walking out the door would give me closure. But it felt nothing like that. Just nostalgia and a longing for things that no longer existed. I knew it would be much harder than I expected to let go of the past. Freedom in the physical doesn't equal freedom in the emotional. Not right on cue, at least.

Delayed.

Delayed.

And I was so impatient to be free of him and the memories.

As I drove away, I continued looking back at my home, surprised at the feeling of loss. I knew nothing had been lost—it was all within me, memories and ideas, faith and hope—but still, the sadness swept over me. Memories, ideas, faith, and hope. The catalysts for creation.

This is where it all began. And this is where it all ended?

I am the Alpha and the Omega. What did that even mean in my reality? It had been a dream, long ago, a voice in my head and symbols flashing before my eyes. Alpha and Omega. I am the Alpha and the Omega. I am the beginning and the end. It all starts with me and ends with me. That's when I knew it wasn't over yet. I was not at my end. *But this moment was meant to be my final release from the past. This is the end.* I convinced myself to let it all go.

"Goodbye," I whispered.

EXAMINING THE PAST

Journal Entry

What I have learned from past relationships:

My expectations are not too high—I want what I want, but at the same time I sometimes think I shouldn't want certain things. Wanting makes me weak.

I can love unconditionally.

I can be vulnerable, and it made me feel free.

Ask questions, ask questions, lots of questions. This is good, but the other lesson is not to be too direct with your questions—it sometimes causes others pain.

To speak my truth, even if painful. This is huge.

To trust myself, to trust my intuition. To see the warnings and accept them instead of ignoring them because of the emotions I feel. However, the other side to this is:

To still be fearless and take risks, a leap of faith, despite the possible issues. Is this good or bad? The beauty of the experience is a choice, so I could choose to enjoy the beauty despite knowing there would be pain.

I want the person who fulfills my non-negotiable list. It's not wrong to want that.

I can't always fix everything. People must fix themselves. They must want to. And it is not up to me to convince them to heal. It is what it is, and I can't control them or their decisions.

I'm beautiful inside and out. The outer beauty, that which I used to make myself feel better and get attention, is nothing, really, except a fleeting glimpse. The inside is the real beauty.

I don't need approval from others, including lovers. I can be myself and accept myself. If they don't approve, they can go to hell.

Life is too short to waste time on things that keep us stuck or unhappy. That doesn't mean it is easy to move on from them. It is damned hard. If someone isn't giving you what you want and need, then move on.

Moving on from heartbreak is much harder than I expected. I learned that I needed to work on cutting loose, even after the words were said and actions were taken.

I can become obsessed with looking at the past and the what-ifs. Should I have done something differently? I've done what I've done. I can learn from what I've done, but it can't be changed.

I am stronger than I thought.

Intuition can get murky when your emotions get involved. You can feel something intuitively, but if you are emotionally a mess, those intuitive feelings will be off.

Pay attention to my spirit guides. They are giving me messages. Some I've ignored and misinterpreted because of my emotions.

My thoughts and emotions are interconnected. Each affects the other. It's a very difficult loop to get out of.

I love myself. I've learned to love myself, flaws and all.

I can survive change, especially change that I don't want.

I can say no.

I ought to give without expecting anything in return. But it is wonderful to get something back.

I have helped people along the way.

You can't change people. Even with passion and words of advice, even if you feel you are right.

Rejection impacted me significantly. My fear of rejection and abandonment needed more work. I realized what I needed was self-love. I wanted to be loved and accepted, and rejection makes me feel as if I wasn't good enough.

Sometimes there aren't any answers. Sometimes things just happen. We can't always know the why. All we can do is explore our actions in a situation and look at our emotions and why we reacted a certain way. Why did we meet? To learn and grow must be enough. That is the why. Beyond that, a mystical reason may never be known.

Healing takes time.

Sex is important, but it doesn't define the relationship. If it does, then it is just sex. The energy shared between people can be beautiful, but more beautiful if there are deeper emotions.

I'd chosen the broken people. Emotionally unavailable men. Non-committal. Was I reliving the past or just protecting myself from deep emotions? I knew from the beginning these broken people wouldn't work out. I chose them. But why? I was blind to others' faults.

Living in the moment is crucial.

I love those intimate moments where you are so close you feel like you are one.

I want to be respected, not belittled.

Confidence is important.

I want integrity, justice, and a willingness to help those who need help. I want an understanding of the injustice in the world, and I care about the rights of others. To accept all people and ideas, discouraging hate and bigotry.

Some of my beliefs about being strong and independent were wrong. It doesn't mean being in charge in a relationship or playing games. Everything should be done from the heart.

I must not be fearful to be who I am or express my spirituality.

The pain was okay, because it brought me to a place of healing. Bad things are good.

I can achieve my dreams.

I trust. I learned to trust even if that trust had been broken before.

I need to watch out for toxic codependent relationships.

I'd like to know what he learned. Why does it matter?

The biggest thing I have learned?

I'm a professional saboteur.

A CLICHÉ CALLED HOME

Home. What defines exactly what home is? Is it a place? A home could be a physical place filled with our possessions, our mementos, and the material objects we believe define us. Home is more than that. I am more than the art on the walls and the objects I collect or the clothes I wear.

When I decided I needed to get rid of at least half my things before I moved, I held up each item and asked, "Does this give me joy?" Marie Kondo's brilliant idea of decluttering your life by getting rid of everything that did not give you joy, seemed a simple concept, yet a difficult one to follow. I was holding on to far too many things that didn't give me joy. *Dating and men—chuck it in the dumpster. Ditto for the brain and the heart. I could live on intuition alone!*

I discovered that far too many possessions gave me joy. It was probably just nostalgia, which is different—clinging onto things from the past that used to give us joy. I'm different now, and I think the memories associated with a vase give me joy, not the vase itself. *Vase to the dumpster.* Nothing conveys a complete picture of who I am. Even the old photo albums and journals filled with words from the heart are just snapshots of my soul and aren't the whole picture. I'll keep those, though. But I'll get rid of the banal and ugly.

Home is not a place. Home is a feeling. Comfort, simplicity, and a sense of belonging. Love. Peace. Balance.

Even logically understanding all of this, there was an awareness of loss, a hint of sadness, and even homesickness. The moment I drove away from my old house, my home, was more emotional than I expected. I was saying goodbye to many things, some of which I still didn't understand.

While I donated a ton of unnecessary possessions, I also kept too much, too many things I'd decided still filled me with joy. How could so many things give me joy? My glass bottle collection, shells from around the world, and a multitude of feathers I'd collected. Simple, beautiful things I was afraid of losing forever were now in storage. I ended up storing a few boxes in a friend's basement. Twenty-five, to be exact. So just a tad more than a few. I was okay with losing everything that went into my storage pod. The entire pod could disintegrate, and I would be completely okay. I didn't even remember half of what I packed in there. Furniture, boxes of kitchen supplies, linens, and boxes of junk I thought I'd one day need, even though I hadn't used any of the items in years. I felt no anxiety when the driver drove away with a chunk of my life on a truck. Only relief.

I kept some basics: clothing, spiritual accessories, jewelry, some meaningful books, and of course, my journals and notebooks. Just a few other basic necessities, but still too much. I created my stories from those journals and notebooks. Real life is woven together with made-up stories. Mostly fiction, but small hints of reality. I often wrote in pen in wire-bound notebooks. It had to be a certain pen. There's an ease and comfort that comes from writing by hand, the words flow more freely than from the tap-tap-tap of a keyboard, so quick and precise. You're more prone to editing when you type, deleting what you think is too dark or too genuine. Thoughts flow more freely when your hand is flowing. There is little room for self-editing.

Most of these writings were already in my head until they were written in ink and then eventually transferred to my computer. I would not write for months, at least in the traditional way. But I would write in my head. It would all be there when I was ready to put pen to paper. The words would come flowing out. Nothing was ever lost. My talent, or curse, for remembering every detail helped me add to my stories. *Real life makes for the best fiction.*

As I settled into my new life in my new room, I was surrounded by the possessions I presumed had value. I stared at everything. Still too much stuff. Still too much clutter. As I looked around, I was anxious about what I was going to do. Where would I live? Where was I going? What the hell was my path?

I had no answers at that moment. I already missed having my own home, my own space. There, my own space was a small room overflowing with too many boxes and possessions I likely would not ever even use. After looking around, I realized there were only about half a dozen boxes of things with which I could never part. There was very little I needed to start a new life. A new home? I needed freedom, but I had no idea what that meant. I had only been here a few days, and already, I wanted to escape. I wanted to go home.

I kept repeating to myself the overused cliché: *Home is where the heart is. Home is where the heart is.* But my heart felt sad. And lonely. And restless. And I didn't know how to fix it.

THE EMPRESS

I gazed out toward the horizon. There were infinite possibilities, and each path was so different from the one before. Where would each one lead? The future was murky, unseen. I could only see what was in front of me at eye level. I spun around, and the view was the same. Endless sky and clouds below. I felt I could walk right out onto them, taking soft, cushioned steps away from the mountaintop. I couldn't see what lay below. The paths down the mountain led to unknown futures. I couldn't foresee all the possible outcomes. I wanted to close my eyes and leap, running as fast as I could down the mountain, moving forward and letting fate decide where I would land.

However, I felt that I must make the choice. I was in control. And while I felt empowered, brave, and confident, I also felt this was a significant pivotal moment, perhaps the pivotal moment, that would bring me to the place.

Whatever the place was…It nearly paralyzed me with fear, knowing my next step could determine the rest of my future.

I wanted love back in my life, but I knew I wasn't ready. There was still a sinewy thread, stretched almost to the point of tearing, that kept me in some way connected to him. It was normal, I knew. Logical. Although most of the soul-bound connection had been released, some small bits still needed to be released, cutting the cord forever. What was the feeling? Was it painful regret or fear of the future? I wasn't sure. Would the end of the connection constitute an ultimate release and then offer completion of letting him go? Why was I still afraid to let him go?

The thought shocked me—there was still some fear of releasing him! I wasn't afraid of being alone…or was I? My moments of solitude were precious, and I wanted to grasp my life and mold the future on my terms, making decisions that couldn't be influenced by connections. Was it the fear of giving up hope? Sometimes when we wish for something so deeply, and it becomes an obsession, it consumes every molecule in our bodies and souls like a disease. Bits and pieces remain despite our best efforts of cleansing. So the remnants needed to be cleared out—that much was obvious. I could still choose a path and continue to heal while I moved forward. Instant healing was unrealistic. I knew it would take time.

I knew what I wanted. At that moment, with the realization that there was still healing to be done, I knew the path was to keep fighting, to continue living and understanding my story. My story was not complete. I'd found my passion. There was nothing else I wanted to do. Despite the risks and my impractical and perhaps foolish approach.

I took the leap of faith, not even looking for a path on firm ground but instead flying with faith and trust into the unknown. The feeling of freedom, of feeling the breath of the Universe surrounding and protecting me, was reassuring. I had chosen my path—an unmarked, unknown, and unplotted flight plan. Walking wasn't an option. The safe, grounded path wasn't an option. I ignored the naysayers, the practical advisors, and the cynics, and I followed my heart.

Like a hawk, I will fly.

SLAMMING THE DOOR TO THE PAST

Everything moved too slowly. Time felt as if it were an infinite stream of sand in an ever-expanding hourglass. I needed to do something. I couldn't write. I hadn't written anything in my journal in a long time except for one story—maybe the start of another book, or maybe something that would stay buried in my journal forever. My character was very confused. She didn't know what she wanted. Like me. I had expected a lot of progress. Emotional turmoil is a great catalyst. *I should be writing.* I perceived it as monumental—my leap into the unknown.

I should be writing about it.

I forced myself to write. Nothing came out. *Today I ate an apple and felt happy.* Banal and ordinary, an inner life stifled by a lack of drama. Eventually, I simply allowed myself to flow. This was a huge step for me, to release the pressure of writing and just flow into my new life. I took a break from chronicling the lives of complicated women. I only wrote things that were unimportant to me. Ghostwriting romance novels, earning a little money spinning cliched plots. The words on the page were just a story, nothing deeply significant, nothing that would change the world. The story of a woman who was guaranteed a happily-ever-after ending. A romance novel without a happy ending was sacrilegious. I was still undecided about whether I should grant my character a corny happy ending. It just didn't feel right to me. She probably deserved it, but was that reality? Real life is not like a romance novel. *Unfortunately.*

There was no order in my life anymore. I wasn't responsible for anything. I wanted freedom, and now that it was here, I didn't know what to do with it. I went for long walks or watched the sunset. Friends, family, the usual…boredom. I had nothing about which to organize, plan, or obsess. It wasn't enough. I felt as if I was avoiding something. Subconsciously, I probably knew what the something was, but I didn't want to face it. *What do I still need to face? In my mind, I had confronted everything I needed to.* I didn't want to ask my heart for fear of starting an argument. These next few months would be about me enjoying everything until the last possible moment of life. Maybe I would find answers, maybe not. Either way, it would be okay.

My heart must have been listening. It chimed in and asked me if I was healed, and if I was honestly, finally moving on. *Did it even matter?* I wanted to believe yes, I was healed and ready for a new life. What if I was wrong? Like last time. Like every time. I was still broken. It was taking so long for me to feel whole that I wasn't even sure what wholeness meant anymore. Returning to my old self, I realized I wasn't even an authentic person back then, before I met him. But I'd been happy. Kind of. Maybe. I'd been confident. Maybe. I wasn't sure who I had been my entire life. I felt like a character in a book.

I did identify with a few of my creations. When my character in my first book finally reached the end of her journey, the top of the mountain, I thought that was the end. She was free, so I was free. I believed I understood everything

I needed to understand. But there were still many things I didn't see. For me, the journey didn't end on top of the mountain. While my character was free, I was still bound to some other unknown ending.

A few years ago, out of nowhere, he came back into my life. Just as I was finally feeling free. Just as I finally thought I had moved on. *Of course. Isn't that how it always happens?*

I would never have let him back in after everything. It was accidental. A case of mistaken identity. I received a text in the middle of the night from someone I had broken up with recently. I wasn't sure why he was texting me. We weren't enemies, nor were we friends. He said he needed to talk to me right away. He asked if he could call. I wasn't interested in talking to him. I could've ignored it. But he was a nice guy. I had broken up with him, and I knew he was hurt. He was too clingy. But guilt made me do it.

Reluctantly, I told him to go ahead and call. I didn't feel like talking to him, and I knew it would probably mean a circular conversation and some firm words. But I wanted to get it over with. My phone rang a few seconds later, and after my "Hello?" I heard *his* voice. It wasn't *clingy man*—it was *him. My man*, as I often referred to him, although he was never mine. I felt awful when I realized my mistake. *I should have deleted his contact info*. His first name was too common. I never expected him to reach out. For all I knew, he was dead. I didn't think he would ever have the courage to reach out. I had labeled him a coward. *Never say never.*

I didn't want to speak to him. But I did. I felt I had no choice. I was too nice. I didn't want to see him. But I did. I did have a choice, but I was too weak. He said he wanted to be friends. *Finally, can we be friends?* I thought I was ready to be friends. I didn't think the words "just friends," because to me to be *friends* would have been the best imaginable scenario. Being lovers wasn't possible. But friendship might be. I was hopeful for some sort of closure. But still…it was risky.

So we became friends. For an entire month. Perhaps the shortest friendship in history. In the beginning, all seemed well. I thought that finally, we could be comfortable friends. We talked easily about many things. Not about our relationship. That would've been too much. Not surprisingly, things soon turned complicated. I was always looking for answers. Always wanting to know the *why* of everything. The more we talked, and the more things seemed way too normal, the more I felt I needed answers from him. I asked him many complicated questions. He didn't answer most of them. He just shrugged as if he didn't know the answers. I let it go. No point. *He is still the same. I am still the same.*

We said a forgettable goodbye and he drove away, and that was the last time I ever heard from him.

As I watched him drive away, I realized I still had expectations. I was sad. Maybe heartbroken all over again. I still wanted him. I was still wrong about many things. I discovered I still held a kernel of hope that he had changed. It was tiny, but it was there, even though I tried to deny it. Part of me thought he may have wanted more from me. You don't call people or text them in the middle of the night just because you want to be friends.

I had asked him, "Why are you here?"

"I want to be friends," he'd replied.

I knew he was lying.

He claimed he didn't want anything romantic. But then why those late-night calls and all the visits? Maybe he just wanted sex, but he never made a move. It seemed very clear to me that he wanted more than friendship. *Why are you here?* I momentarily thought he did want me. I was wrong. Again. The same mistakes, over and over. I couldn't believe I kept falling for false hope. After he left, I spent a lot of time going back and forth in my mind, trying to find answers.

What had I done wrong? He was the one who'd done wrong. I shouldn't have asked questions. He should have answered… And so it went, as I tried to find blame somewhere.

I spent too much time thinking about him and our messy connection. All the what-ifs. My mistakes, his mistakes. What if I had been more patient? What if I had tried harder to understand his perspective? I philosophized about love and loss. Then the old pain resurfaced, and I found myself back at the beginning of my healing. Starting over, back to being trapped in my thoughts, wanting him and wanting to release my love for him at the same time. Searching again for the strength to release him. *It had taken me so long to be free.* It was frustrating.

I finally just told myself to stop thinking and obsessing about it. *Just stop,* I willed myself. I knew there was nothing I could do. I had done all that I could.

Just stop. There is no going back to hell. Let the coward go.

With those words and a lot of strength, I took full control of my thoughts and pushed away my emotions. I would not be sad or happy about him. I would be neutral. I wanted answers, but I knew I would never find them. And I had to tell myself it was okay. The confusion would always remain, and I didn't need to understand anything else.

Whether it was a soul connection or a toxic connection didn't matter. I needed to let go of everything. I'd been wrong about many things. And I was also right. Although I'd been wrong about the outcome—I'd thought we would be together—I was right about the emotions I felt. I loved him and always would. And he would still permeate and stain my thoughts on my weakest days. I didn't know for how much longer I could fight this. It may be far in the future before I could let him go. At least my future was short. For now, I would block everything out.

HOPE IS A DANGEROUS THING

What did I hope for in my new, albeit temporary, life? I didn't want to hope for anything. I wanted to simply glide and flow. I would take my trip. I would have an adventure. In the past, I'd had so much hope, and I clung to that hope for too long. It wasn't even visible to me. It was deeply entrenched in my subconscious, a part of me that still had hope that he would heal and return whole. Yes, I still thought about him and I continued to hope he would come back a changed man. It wasn't even anything I thought about clearly—just a sense that I was still bound in some way I couldn't understand. Despite all the inner work I had already done, I still felt this way. I didn't want to lose hope. It wasn't even that I didn't want to lose him. It was the loss of hope that was the most painful.

Hope is what keeps us going. Keeps us moving forward. Without hope…Well, I wasn't so sure hope even mattered. *I hope, I hope, I hope*…empty words full of empty promises.

I met a man soon after my final meeting with him. *Final* final meeting? I had no idea. But I met a man. I felt an instant connection. Not as deep as I had with him, but I was shocked. I wasn't expecting *that* to happen again. The moment it happened, this connection with this new person, I felt lighter, as if a heavy burden had been released.

What was that burden? *Fear.* Fear that I would never have a connection like I'd had with him again. The fear that I'd again be rejected. That I'd spend the rest of my life alone. I carried this within me, and it did more than weigh me down. It crushed me and blocked me from making decisions about my life. I was stuck. I'd been waiting without even knowing. I'd been waiting for him to come back. Still hoping. Even after everything. *How pathetic is that?*

HOPELESS

So even though I was supposed to be the Empress at the top of the mountain, I was terrified. I had to decide. To leap or to go back on the same path I'd taken to reach the top.

Do I want to hope?

If I took the old path, the familiar path of too much hope, I would set myself up for disappointment. Regret. Pain. At the same time, I needed to hope for something. I was tired of wanting him. Tired of false hope. Tired of being stuck. Tired of thinking about it. I had jumped into a new life. I had taken the path less traveled. Independent and strong, I wanted to stand on my own for a while.

And there appeared this new person. I was scared of having too much hope and releasing the old hope. It was complicated. I was also afraid of being alone, of living the rest of my life without a man, without love. I had learned to love myself unconditionally. However, I still craved—no, needed—love from someone else.

Was it okay? Was this normal? That I wanted or needed someone's love? I kept thinking I needed to be independent and strong, and that it was not okay to need or want romantic love. I liked him. I instantaneously felt something, similar to what I had with my old love. And at the same time, I was hesitant.

I'm not scared, I told myself.

That's when it hit me. I *was* scared. Scared of rejection. Abandonment. I still had issues I needed to deal with. I liked this new man. But the more I told myself I wasn't scared, the more I understood that I was. I'd built a wall around myself, to protect myself. I wasn't going to be hurt again. Funny, those were the same words my past lover had spoken to me when we first met. Words I'd ignored.

I'm not scared. We had switched places. And I was now the one who was afraid to be vulnerable with a man despite my desire for a relationship and love. This completely stopped me in my tracks. I realized that was the reason I had been holding on to him. If I held onto him, it would be impossible for me to move forward with anyone else. I had deceived myself into believing I was waiting for him. I woke up. The person I most wanted was also who I was using as protection from future pain. The idea of our special connection was a security blanket. If I held onto false hope, I never had to surrender to anyone again. *Because he was coming back.*

Of course, at the time, I wasn't thinking so clearly. I was just fearful and impulsive. I was worried about what this new man would think of me. What if I told him my deep, dark secrets?

Hello, new man. By the way, for several years I've been obsessed with my old lover. I even wrote a book that was sort of about him. I've shared my cringey pain with the world. And yes, I still love him and am holding onto hope that he'll come back.

He would be gone in an instant. I didn't want to be rejected again. So, yet again, I edited myself. I crossed out what I didn't want him to see. I pretended to be balanced. To be something I was not. I molded myself into the person I thought he would want me to be.

Did he even like me? I wondered if I should care. Should I love him? Was heartbreak coming my way? I rewired my brain and forced it to tell my heart to stop feeling. Change the feelings. No—block the feelings. *Do not become attached.* I would take complete control and be cold and aloof. I would do the rejecting. I was ready to send him on his way. This was the new me. Controlled, cold, and distant.

I vowed never to see that new man again. He reached out, but I ghosted him.

Goodbye from the Ice Queen.

THE TIGER

Journal Entry

She saw him out of the corner of her eye, slowly emerging from the jungle, deliberately and quietly stretching his legs, creeping into the open field. He was huge—the largest tiger she had ever seen. Despite her fear, she was moved by his beauty. His brilliant orange and black stripes shone in the moonlight.

Her fear was muted. She should have been terrified, but for some reason, she was surprisingly calm. *Okay.* She was just going to stand here for a minute. She kept looking at the tiger. His eyes were locked on her, and he was moving forward quite slowly. It was hard to discern if he was moving at all.

Then she saw it. A flicker in his eye. His expression told her that he was coming for her. He looked hungry.

She wanted to run but wasn't sure where to go. She looked down and saw a rifle in the grass. She had no idea where it had come from. Reaching down, she picked it up and pointed it at the tiger. Looking through the scope, she fixed the sight on him. The tiger stopped. As she was deciding whether to pull the trigger, she was overcome by an uneasy feeling of regret. She brought the rifle down to her side at stared at the tiger. She sensed he would not attack her. *Why is he here? Does he have something to tell me?* She slowly moved toward the tiger, hoping he would answer her questions.

Everything started to dissolve—the scenery, the tiger, as she was pulled back to the real world by the sound of lawnmowers outside her window.

She opened her eyes and realized it was all a dream. *Ugh. Nothing like being awoken from a dream that was turning meaningful.* The tiger had to wait. She had to finish packing for her trip.

SELF-PRESERVATION

Alan, the arrogant and late first date on my quest, was persistent. He kept reaching out. There I was, trying to figure out my life, and he kept annoying me. I finally decided to reply. I could've blocked him or continued to ignore him, but I felt bad doing that.

Should I give him a chance?

I had worked hard to get to where I was, to reach a point where I didn't care what people thought of me. *I am fearless,* I told myself. Did I need to be myself or someone else? I was letting that freedom go because of fear of loneliness. I told myself, *Enough*! I am who I am, and I love who I am. I am going to be myself and not try to change even minor things to make him think I am in line with what he wants. The chameleon was dead. He could see those things about me that he doesn't agree with, and he could decide whether I was worth it or not.

I was unsure about him, and yet I hoped he would make me permanently forget the old love, the pain. Prevent it from returning at inopportune times. *Was that enough*?

My brain said *no*, and my heart said *yes*. My heart wanted instant healing. Could Alan make me forget? Maybe there would be some healing for me in the process. Being with him would somehow help me understand myself better and how to better deal with my old pain. My mind said, *Running into the arms of another man as a means of healing old wounds does nothing but mask the pain.* My heart said, *But the pain will go away.* It was a tie as they battled back and forth.

Maybe I'd judged him too quickly. Maybe we had a deeper connection not yet discovered. Those were all words from my heart. *Maybe there was a possibility for something more.*

He was arrogant, said the mind. *No. I made a judgment,* said the heart.

How much did I like him? I was lukewarm. If I liked him, wouldn't I have jumped in already, like always? I had to approach things cautiously, without being cold and closed off either. Balancing both heart and mind, I knew what I needed was to heal. *Is he the right choice for me right now?*

CHOICES

I knew I had to make some big decisions. *Choices.* Choice was my word of choice. I knew I craved a new environment, a new life. A new beginning, a new attitude, maybe even a new *me*. It was time to take a leap of faith—but where? How? I was scared. Scared of not having both feet on the ground, scared of change, scared of uncertainty. The unknown. Being seen as a failure. Even though this was a choice, to move out and become a vagabond, I still felt that people would look at me and see a failure. I needed to prove my success. Do something adventurous.

I have to stop worrying about what people think. The only thing that was holding me back at the moment was *Where do I go from here?* What will happen to this new potential love? I had no idea. But I just wanted freedom.

Freedom from responsibility. Freedom from worry. Freedom from the past emotional connections that were still embedded in my soul. I needed to release the feeling of being bound to him. It wasn't happening in the way I expected and was taking a lot more time than I'd anticipated. I longed for freedom. *Freedom from myself.*

I hated the fact that I still thought about him, that I still felt the pain from the loss. Although it was muted, it was still there. A longing for something impossible. I didn't have hope. I knew it was over and done, and I needed to move on. Hope is what nearly killed me in the first place. I was realistic, but my emotions still tried to overpower me. I fought them every step of the way. I refused to accept the fact that I still wanted him. That I still needed healing. Most of the time I was balanced, and those feelings only really surfaced when I tried to meet a new man. *Like now.* In those moments, I felt a loss of hope, that I would never fall in love again, and that no other man nor connection would ever compare to him and the bond we'd had. Even if it was all in my mind. *To him, I was probably nothing. It was so easy for him.*

All I wanted was to erase him from my heart, from my mind. Mind erasure. *I wished it existed. I would forget I ever met him.* Those were the moments when I would become the most unstable, knowing logically what was wrong, knowing what I needed to do, yet emotionally being unable to release. The thoughts caused the emotions. The emotions caused the thoughts. An endless loop of mind and heart, forever triggering each other, stuck on repeat.

When I learned of my impending death, all of this should have been diminished, right? Who cares about anything else when you're going to die? A man is just a man. *Maybe I should just reach out to him and ask him to spend the next year with me as my last dying wish.* I thought about it. Honestly. With all this conflict, plus my new homelessness, maybe it was just time to leave. Forget the new man I'd met. Go away, discover, and have an adventure. Free myself once and for all from hope and desire. It was a crumb of hope that I hardly noticed most of the time. But it was enough to prevent me from moving forward in my life without hesitation. As hard as I tried, I couldn't make it go away. I couldn't understand why it remained. And I wanted it gone before I died.

As I grew more restless, my landscape also grew foggier. The heaviness of the fog engulfed me. I wanted to move, go, and get away, but things were murky. I had no idea where to go or what to do. Finally, when the fog lifted after a few days of sitting in a daze, I saw clearly what I most feared—that I would long for him for the rest of my life and remain alone, lonely, and unable to meet anyone else or fall in love because of my stuckness. There was no other man who could take his place. Ever. I would never feel that way again. I desperately needed to get unstuck.

SETTLING INTO MOVEMENT

The order of things was confusing. I can't remember the exact details. I just jumped into my car. I had no idea where I was going or what I was looking for. Not answers. I had too many of those. I needed a purpose. I was so excited about the trip. But I was also a tad nervous. I always planned everything and did tons of research before each trip I'd ever taken. Left no stone unturned. Prepared for all sorts of unexpected possibilities. There would be none of that this time. And I was alone. I could be murdered or raped. Or both. I could get hopelessly lost and run out of gas in a remote location and die of starvation. I pushed those fears aside, packed my car with too many things, half of which I probably wouldn't even use, and drove away. I didn't even say goodbye to Alan. *Goodbye, new man*. I realized I didn't care at all.

"You forgot the pepper spray!" my friend said as she ran out of the house.

I wasn't even sure I wanted it, but I thanked her and put it in my glove compartment. She was worried, so I needed to reassure her. Intuitively, I knew everything would be fine. I would be fine. I wouldn't die or get injured. Even if I did, so what? My mantra was *Everything will be okay*. I certainly hoped I wasn't wrong—a rarity, but as I knew, sometimes my intuition was off if my emotions overpowered my sense of knowing. But that was only with men. Everything else was pure trust. I breathed in—no emotion, just pure intuition. Yes, everything would be okay. As long as I didn't love again.

I drove off, down the driveway. South. Just south. I decided to go to North Carolina. Maybe the mountains. I'd always wanted to go to Asheville. Before I'd become cynical, when I used to believe in everything, I'd wanted to go and explore the energy vortexes that were supposedly in the mountains surrounding the city. Maybe that's where I would find my answers. The farther I drove, the freer I felt, and my mind turned to thoughts of my "purpose."

Many asked why, and I always replied—*adventure*. I knew that was only part of the answer but going into detail and explaining myself seemed pointless. Part of it was my feeling of insanity, the overthinking that played in my head when I was searching for answers that didn't have a logical solution.

My intuition told me to. That was my answer. This was something I had to do for reasons yet unknown. *Just flow*, I told myself. This was my personal, private reason. I kept it to myself, not wanting to be judged. It was complicated to explain, my quest for questions. I only knew I had to go.

TOO MUCH BAGGAGE

There was too much stuff. Just way too much. I carried things I *may* need in the future. Just like everything I'd been carrying from my life. The emotions, the pain, the baggage that had grown overwhelming, and that I towed along wherever I went. That baggage was a lot more difficult to leave behind—all those little "just in case" things. Those in my car, those things would've been easy to leave behind. Perhaps they were all unnecessary, but I thought I needed them at the time. A sleeping bag in case I wanted to camp. However, I knew there was no way I would have camped by myself. Plus, I didn't have a tent. I wasn't camping either by myself or with anyone else without a tent. I hadn't slept in the great outdoors since I was a kid. I loved nature but also loved being warm and having a real bathroom. Oh, and the bears. I was afraid of being torn to shreds by bears. However, I was adventurous, so I needed a sleeping bag.

I also brought a plastic bin full of books. A great pile of books that had sat on my nightstand for years, that I planned to read one day. *Someday.* I packed them in a bin because I knew I'd have lots of time for reading. I don't think I opened that bin at all during my entire trip. But I had it, just in case. I threw in some blank notebooks, too, for more writing and journaling. Some paint and paintbrushes. Just in case.

I had enough toiletries and snacks to last for weeks. Just in case there were no grocery stores on my trip. I wasn't too hard on myself about that. It was not quite the end of the pandemic, and I needed to be cautious. I was trying to avoid going into too many places. I was still afraid of dying of Covid back then, and I wore my mask all the time. The less I ventured into public places, the safer I would be. I didn't want to die quite yet. I had more to do and preferred to let my death come naturally.

I didn't realize how much stuff I had until I made my first stop in the mountains just outside Asheville, NC. I arrived and I unloaded everything I needed, about four or five bags and bins. Clothes, food, and other necessities. And somehow my car was still full. *I didn't need anything else.* No sleeping bag, no books, no extra towels, batteries, tools, or my Himalayan salt lamp. They were just along for the ride. The baggage gave me comfort while at the same time weighing me down.

A CABIN IN THE WOODS

I scanned the landscape from the front porch. It was beautiful. Quiet. Secluded. Not another person in sight. But I had done something foolish. And I was scared. I'd rented a remote and secluded cabin in the mountains. I had imagined myself writing on the porch and sipping my wine. No—something stronger. Whiskey or scotch. No, coffee would keep me alert. Alcohol would just make me write things I didn't want to write about.

As I made my way down the long, gravel road I wondered how the hell was I going to sleep that night. I feared being alone. I always had. *I'm crazy. Who does something like this?* I was a woman traveling alone. But I was determined. I did it because it scared me. *I'm not avoiding those things I fear anymore. I'm facing my fears.*

I walked in with my mask on and sprayed the entire place with an all-natural disinfectant. I hated the smell of Lysol, and I hoped the lack of an actual disinfecting ingredient in my all-natural spray wouldn't make a difference. I quickly threw the pillows off the bed and grabbed my pillows from the car. I checked the sheets to make sure they were clean, ripping off the comforter. I sprayed the bed. I brought in my air purifier. I turned it on but kept my mask on for a bit longer. I was fearful of getting Covid.

And the fear of being alone in the woods. Eventually, I would stop being so paranoid. But I needed to be in the beginning.

After I settled in, I took a short walk around the property. *Ten acres of quiet, secluded natural beauty. Not a soul in sight.* I verified that. The closest house I could see was at least a mile away, so there were other souls in sight. Just not within shouting for help distance. *I wanted this. I'd asked for this solitude.* But I was scared. *Be careful what you wish for.*

I ate in since food was too far a drive, and at that point, it was getting dark, and I was lazy. *I wish I had some alcohol. Should've packed alcohol, too.* That was a necessity. More than a salt lamp anyway.

After a spectacular sunset, darkness crept in slowly. I sat on my porch, fighting off the bugs and drinking my…tea. *Sigh.* I heard a crack in the woods. No, a crunch. Maybe a snap. Like someone stepping on a branch. I jumped up and ran toward the door. I didn't run into the house because I was determined to be brave. I peered into the woods, squinting, but it was too dark. My flashlight was in the car. And my pepper spray. *Damn.*

Luckily, there was a flashlight in the kitchen drawer. Probably for chickens like me. *Do I look or not look?* I wasn't sure. I wanted to lock myself in the house, but at the same time, what if a serial murderer was hiding in the woods and he killed me in my sleep? I suppose I had to find out.

I slowly crept onto the porch, a flashlight in one hand and my phone in the other, ready to call 911. I realized I couldn't go too far, since I didn't have cell service and the Wi-Fi was weak. Maybe I'd be able to see from the edge of the porch. I took two more cautious steps toward the tree line and pointed the flashlight into the woods. Nothing. I couldn't see a thing. It was pitch black and the flashlight wasn't strong enough. *Crack.*

Shit. This time, I ran into the house, slamming and bolting the door shut. I just stood there, wondering what to do next. I had no idea what was out there, but I wasn't taking any chances. I turned on every single light in the house and every floodlight outside. Bright. I was the brightest light on the mountainside. Blinding. *No one would dare attack me now.* I quickly checked the windows. Locked. I went to my bedroom and locked the door and sat up in my bed.

Now what? I sat and listened. No more cracks in the woods. It was probably just a raccoon. *Hopefully not a bear.* I told myself to stop being a chicken. There was nothing to be afraid of.

I was tired and soon fell into a deep sleep, cell phone in one hand, flashlight in the other.

CALL OF THE WILD

In the middle of the night, I opened my eyes to a brilliant, blinding light. I didn't understand how I'd even been able to sleep; one small salt lamp was fine, but this was too much. When I was a kid, I was afraid of the dark, and this followed me to adulthood. My salt lamp was my adult night light. So I guess it was a necessity after all. *But this—too bright.* It was time to turn out the lights. I felt comfortable, and my fear had eased. I chided myself for my ridiculous behavior.

I went around the house to every room, flipping light switches off, and turning off lamps. That's when I heard the bloodcurdling scream. It sounded as if it was coming from right outside the back door. It made me jump out of my skin, but I tried to remain calm. I held my breath for a few seconds.

1, 2, 3, 4…I'm not screaming. I'm not scared.

Then another scream. Someone was being murdered on the porch. I knew it. And then they would come for me. A person? A bear? Bigfoot? A stampeding cow (I'm scared of cows)?

I had to get upstairs. My phone was upstairs. I had to call 911.

What the hell is my address?

I heard the screeching again. This time it was quieter. Or maybe I was calmer.

I'm not afraid. I'm not afraid. I kept telling myself these words, yet I was afraid.

I had no choice but to face my fears. I slowly crept toward the door and very, very carefully pulled apart one of the slats in the blinds.

I'm not afraid.

I didn't find a mass murderer on the porch. Nor bigfoot. And of course, not a cow.

Right at the bottom of the stairs were two foxes. Maybe one was calling the other with its screeching? I knew fox calls sometimes sounded like screams. Although I had heard them, I'd never heard one so close. They looked relaxed and happy, touching noses. They were making small sounds now, speaking in secret fox language. Maybe one of them had been lost, and the cries were cries of sorrow and grief. Like humans, the loss of their lover inflicted them with such pain they cried out for their mate in the darkness of night, hoping, praying, they would return. Unlike humans, the lost and wandering fox heard the call and immediately returned.

I'm so cynical now. The animal world was more loyal. Logically, I knew it wasn't true. Humans are every bit as sorrowful and regretful, every bit as lonely, and every bit as prone to crying out in the night for their lovers. The only difference was that the human lover couldn't hear, no matter how hard we cry. There was no instinct or intuitive pulling to be with someone. Most people felt nothing and moved on in their lives, leaving the past behind without ever looking back.

I wish I could do that. I can't stand that I think about things too much, nor that I want things too much. It isn't right, fair, or normal. *I'm crazy. I want to be a fox. Crazy like a fox. Isn't that a TV show?*

I tried to sleep, but my thoughts drifted to love. It's rare. True love is rare. All these people who claimed to be in love, that wasn't real. How could it be? It's so complex and difficult, *and* so many people are deeply afraid. True, unconditional love takes a strong, fearless person. Who has the strength to keep trying? If so many people are afraid, maybe it's not something we should search for or fight for. Hope for. With so much apprehension and fear, why do we bother? Maybe love is an illusion, something that keeps us bound to one another, a biological attraction to bring forth more imperfect humans into the world. Pheromones.

I think most people settle. They reach a point, and they take whatever they can grab out of desperation. Is that more realistic than waiting for the perfect person? *Nobody is perfect! Nobody is even close to ever being perfect.* If I wanted a perfect man, I should have walked past every single man I had ever dated over the last few years. But I liked them imperfect. Broken. Too broken. *We're all broken.* We're all imperfect, but we dream in twos. Two foxes, two owls, duality, and mirrors. Maybe I'm the only broken one and everyone else is perfect. I see lovers pairing off around me and myself adrift, lonely, and wondering—*What is wrong with me?*

THE MAGIC MOUNTAIN

After a glorious sunrise with very little sleep and several cups of coffee, I was on my way to meet my guide. I had one more full day and had arranged for a guided hike. I was anxious about hiking alone. You know, murderers and rapists in the woods. And bears. The thought of being mauled by a bear, killed, or eaten alive, was an irrational fear. I knew that. I had only seen bears from a distance, and they immediately ran in the other direction. Mostly, they ran. Nonetheless, I was afraid.

Maybe my guide would be a ruggedly handsome outdoorsman and we would go on nature adventures together all over the world. I imagined him tall and muscular. Athletic, with a kind but mischievous smile. Mysterious eyes that obscured profound secrets waiting to be discovered. If everything is out in the open, what's the excitement in that? I guess I like them mysterious as well as broken. Probably not the best combination.

I met my guide. He was handsome. Outdoorsy. Confident. Rugged. *Ah!* I was instantly attracted. No wedding ring. This was my chance. Maybe he was the one.

I had told myself I was no longer searching for the perfect man, but here I was again, getting drawn into a fantasy. What was it that kept drawing me to them despite my best efforts to stay celibate? Could I not just see them as people instead of a new conquest or challenge? I understood that I was searching for something that was practically impossible. Logically, I knew searching outside myself wasn't the answer. It was all within. But I couldn't help it. Every man I was attracted to was just another opportunity to find love.

"Hi there," he said.

"Hi," I replied, waving to him.

Are you the man of my dreams? I knew I needed to stop, but I couldn't. I didn't want to miss out on the possibility that he would be the one.

The one what? To save me? Looking for love in too many faces.

We hiked up to a stone circle, a hidden, isolated spot on the mountainside. Not as grand as Stonehenge or other mystical places, but a modest, unassuming place, likely not frequented by many except those who already knew of its existence. My guide told me it was a powerful place, teeming with energy. A vortex, he said. He had felt something powerful several times and enjoyed bringing hikers up there.

"I'm not sure what it is, or what I believe, but there's something here," he said.

He sat on the grass in the center of the stones. I sat next to him. He smiled.

Was he flirting?

I smiled back, then closed my eyes. I tried to feel the energy, hoping it would give me peace and release. A mystical experience that would change my life and maybe provide me with answers. I expected these experiences to be immense and powerful. I repeated my mantra to myself—peace, love, light—over and over, willing myself to experience something mystical and magical.

As hard as I tried, nothing happened. This went on for several minutes. Whatever potent energy was supposed to be present was hidden from me. I wanted to keep going, keep trying to connect, but I somehow knew nothing was going to happen.

I opened my eyes. He was staring at me. I smiled, of course. But I was deeply disappointed. More expectations that hadn't been fulfilled. Something should have happened. *Universe, where are you?*

"So did you feel it?" he asked.

"Yes," I lied.

There was no point telling him the truth and then having a discussion I didn't feel like having. I couldn't connect to anything on a deep level lately. It was all shallow water with no ability to float into tranquility. There would be no release or answers today.

"Great!" he said, overly enthusiastic.

I smiled my seductive smile.

His phone buzzed. He pulled it out of his backpack.

"Sorry, have to check my messages. My wife is organizing a dinner party tonight and I have some errands to run on the way home," he said, turning around to read his messages.

He was married. *Of course he was. All the good ones are taken.*

We spent the rest of the morning climbing to the top of a peak. The beauty of the mountains almost countered the disappointment of the stone circle. I felt the lack of an energetic experience meant something. I was lacking in energy. Something was wrong with my spiritual self. And then, contemplating the lack of potential romance, I wondered whether to continue my quest for the perfect man. He had to be out there, and I wanted to find him before I died. However, like the missing energy, he was probably nowhere to be found. Onward, west. To where I didn't know. Anywhere. As long as it was away from the memories of the past, I was satisfied.

I'M GOING TO GRACELAND

I was still anxious that evening. I wondered if the foxes would return, but now that I'd identified the sound, I wasn't as nervous. Nonetheless, the dark woods still seemed a bit threatening. Other creatures were roaming there. The unknown, dark, mysterious forest. Just like my men. Something to think about. Attracted and simultaneously scared.

As I did throughout my trip, I usually decided the night before where I would go next. This was a big step for me. I was always in control and would plan everything down to every tiny detail before I started something new. This time, I vowed to do things differently. Just a little planning. I would be a wanderer.

I looked at the map and followed the road from Asheville west to Memphis, Tennessee. A song popped into my head immediately. *I'm going to Graceland, Memphis, Tennessee, I'm going to Graceland…* I knew I needed to go to Graceland.

I'd loved Elvis when I was a kid, but only after he'd died. I remember the day, the very moment, my friend knocked on my door and breathlessly told me he'd died. I was just a kid, maybe twelve years old. I don't remember even listening to his music before that, but I knew who he was, and I'm sure I'd heard his songs. I went to my friend's house across the street, and her mother was sitting at the kitchen table in tears. She'd loved Elvis, and said he was her idol. He had a beautiful voice, and he was an angel. So right then and there, I was filled with grief. I sat next to her and joined her in her tears. I'm not even sure why. While I had heard his music, I preferred Shaun Cassidy back then. I would have cried if Shaun had died. It was a surreal and strange experience, mourning Elvis. I spent the next few weeks loving Elvis and listening to his music. I bought a vinyl record, his top hits, and played it over and over, crying every time I heard "Can't Help Falling in Love." Already, back then, I was crying for love.

I still loved his music, and I still felt disappointed that his life had ended too soon. Just like John Lennon, Jim Morrison, and Kurt Cobain. A long list of tragic deaths I sometimes think about. *Only the good die young.* I didn't believe that. And what or who defines *good* anyway? The sadness I felt for Elvis' death wasn't just the childhood empathic tears that belonged to the sadness of my friend's mother. It was a genuine sadness for the loss of a creative spirit.

The Graceland lyrics kept running through my head, *for some reason that I cannot explain, I'm going to Graceland.* Not an Elvis song, but it was enough. Maybe I could commune with the dead Elvis and that would somehow change my life. What had failed in Asheville was maybe meant to happen in Memphis. The song, the endless replay in my head, was a sign.

I was going to Graceland.

I slept about five hours, which was normal so far on my trip. Not nearly enough. I kept waking up, listening for unknown sounds. Thankfully, there was only silence. I slept with fewer lights on though. I was slowly getting accustomed to being alone in the woods. I got up early, had two cups of coffee, and repacked my car. It was still dark as I drove down the gravel road.

I made it a point not to drive at night, but I wanted to get to Memphis before dark, and it was a long drive. That was one of my rules—driving only during daylight. Less chance of anything bad happening. As I drove past the pond and toward the main road, the first thing I noticed was very dense fog. It was still dark and almost impossible to see. I thought about turning around and waiting. After all, I was breaking my no-driving-in-the-dark rule. But I drove on and made a new rule—the no-driving-in-the-dark rule didn't apply in the early a.m. hours because dawn was coming. Technically, it was okay in my mind to be on the road before dawn.

I was anxious. I realized for someone who claimed to be fearless, I had quite a few fears. Hopefully, I would conquer them all on my trip. I didn't turn around. I kept moving forward, even though I couldn't see what lay ahead on the road. There was no going back.

I hoped it would get better on the highway—it didn't. However, I felt safer since the road was wider and it was a divided highway. I didn't have to worry about being hit head-on by another car. I drove slowly, sometimes barely moving more than five miles per hour. Eventually, the sun rose, the fog cleared, and I had beautiful views of the Appalachian Mountains and the Blue Ridge Parkway. I stopped to take a picture, closed my eyes, and inhaled the pure mountain air. I would miss that as I headed west. No more grand mountains until Colorado.

DETOUR

As I headed west through Tennessee, I saw a sign for Chattanooga. I immediately thought about the old song, "Chattanooga Choo Choo." Again, another song looped through my head. Another memory from childhood. It was the theme song for a commercial. Probably trains. I know it was also a song by a big swing band. Or a country singer? The commercial was what was relevant to me. Significant only because I had always wanted a train set when I was little, and every time I saw the commercial, I longed for a miniature train. I would watch it go round and round on an endless loop, going nowhere, but always in motion, carrying imaginary people back and forth. I never got my train set. Instead, I got endless dolls and Barbies, which I did love. They were madly in love with Ken and always lived happily ever after. Although he was missing a vital piece of anatomy, it didn't matter back then. I was just a kid. Barbie had her perfect life, with a man who would always do whatever she wanted and would never leave. Sexless Ken, the perfect, loyal companion. *The perfect man.*

I decided to stop in Chattanooga. It would be short, less than an hour, because I was on a tight schedule. The song led me there, sort of, even though it wasn't a favorite song. I couldn't think of any other songs for Tennessee, except for "The Tennessee Waltz," which didn't inspire me at all.

Maybe what I was looking for would be there. You never know, sometimes those intuitive pings happen for a reason.

I planned to get some coffee, see the river, and set off again. I wanted to get to Graceland. That was more important. *I'm going to Graceland.*

Sometimes we think strange things.

I found parking near the Tennessee River, in the arts district, thinking maybe I would also check out some art galleries. The parking sign was confusing. It said I could park there, except for Sunday between the hours of six a.m. and nine a.m. Strange hours, strange sign. Usually, Sunday was a free parking day. At least back east. I was glad it wasn't Sunday, and there were plenty of spots available. I would only be gone an hour or so, to quickly browse a gallery or two and get my coffee. I needed more coffee. I was feeling drowsy and still had several hours of driving ahead.

Nothing happened as I had envisioned. I shouldn't have been too surprised. So far, not much had been like I had imagined. Coffee was hard to find since most of the coffee shops didn't open until ten a.m. or were closed because of the pandemic. It was eight a.m., and there were very few people on the streets, so I couldn't even ask for help. Finally, I found a coffee shop in a hotel lobby. Crappy coffee, but it was coffee. I'm usually picky about my coffee, but I was desperate and drank it anyway.

I wandered along the waterfront, looking for a small art gallery to explore. None were open yet. As I headed back to my car, I finally spotted a stray open gallery. *Perfect.* I would spend a few minutes looking at the art, maybe finding some sort of sign or synchronicity in a painting or sculpture. *The meaning of life can be found in art and things of beauty.* I was always looking for answers.

"Sorry, you can't bring your coffee or backpack in here," said a woman behind the counter.

"My whole life is in this backpack," I answered.

Well, my valuables were in my backpack. My computer, wallet, jewelry, and whatever else I gave a monetary value to at the time. I never left any of that in the car when I went exploring. I wondered why I'd left my journal in the car. That was more important to me. My jewelry wasn't valuable. I lost things easily and never carried expensive pieces. I didn't change my earrings the entire time and wore the same amethyst necklace. *Just in case*, I thought. I was prepared for anything, including a date.

"You can leave it here with me if you'd like," she said.

I was annoyed and wanted to finish my coffee. I decided it was time to continue west.

"No thank you, another time," I replied.

I returned to where my car was parked, but I couldn't find it. *Did I park somewhere else?* I looked around and suddenly realized why everything was closed. It was Sunday. I had lost track of the days. And now, knowing it was Sunday, I understood why my car was gone. It had been towed. I panicked. Everything was in my car—my clothes, my snacks, and everything else that I thought I needed for my trip.

Where did it get towed to? Why did they move so fast? I was gone less than an hour. And why couldn't I park there on Sunday? So strange. And so ruthless.

When I finally found my car, I had to pay way too much money to get it back. I lost an hour or so in the process since they only took cash and I had to find an ATM. They weren't very pleasant when I complained about the signs. I was happy to continue on my way. *I'm not coming back, Chattanooga.* I hoped I would eventually look back on the experience and laugh, call it an adventure. *In retrospect…* it's difficult to laugh at the moment when bad things are happening. I would laugh later.

I was relieved to get back on the road. I was in control, back on the path that I had chosen. But the Universe wasn't done with me yet.

After I merged onto the highway, I was suddenly boxed in between two semis. I tried to speed up, but then one of them started veering into my lane. The other refused to budge. He saw me, I was sure he did. But he refused to move. I didn't know whether to speed up or slow down. I took quick evasive action, and seeing nobody behind me, I slammed on my brakes, watching the truck swerve into the lane ahead of me. I would surely be dead had I not braked. In retrospect, maybe it wasn't a big deal. But at that moment, I thought I was dead. Smashed between two semis, never knowing the wonders of Graceland. A very close call, and I was only saved by my quick action. It rattled me enough that I had to pull over.

Two bad things in one day, and then I remembered the disappointment of Asheville. No miracles, no answers, and no spiritual meaning to anything. I pulled over and cried. I was scared, and I wanted to go home. I had no deep epiphanies, no life-changing experiences yet. And I was alone. Only conflict. I didn't think I could continue. Were these signs of some sort telling me to go back? *No. Maybe?* I didn't know. I hated when bad things happened. *Life is a balance of good and bad.* I only wanted good, though.

I needed to keep going. Keep going forward, keep going west, and things would improve. I couldn't give up. I would do it, and I could do it alone. *Strength and perseverance.* I kept repeating aloud to myself, *You can do it. You are strong.*

I knew I was strong. And I knew I could do it. But I did feel very alone with nowhere to escape to for safety. I had no choice. My intuition kept pulling me west. Toward what, I didn't know. And even if I wanted to go home, I wasn't going back. That was in the past. And besides, home was not a place for me anymore.

RAINBOWS
AND UNICORNS

Journal Entry

I used to be rainbows and unicorns.
Everything was beautiful, even the pain and ugliness.
I could find the silver lining in everything that happened.
Everything would be okay.
Everything happens for a reason.
There's good in everyone.
If you believe in something deeply enough, you can make it happen.
Wishes can come true.
I was filled with love.
What changed?
Disappointment, loss, and grief.
The destruction of rainbows, the murder of unicorns.

BY THE SIDE
OF THE ROAD

The Airbnb I booked advertised peace—a serene, tranquil farm setting far from the hustle and bustle of Memphis. I was tricked. My expectations were dashed. I was beginning to realize how often I imagined or had visions of what things would be like in the future. Always rosy, always rainbows and unicorns. Too much positive thinking? Toxic positivity, they called it. I believed in everything, including that he and I would be together one day. I felt it, deep in my gut. I never had any doubts in the past about him or anything else. Had I deceived myself, creating a fantasy in my head?

After it was done, I was so angry at myself for trusting my gut. It never failed me, and yet, it seemed everything turned sour, and he was gone. He'd left me, abandoned me. It wasn't until later that I realized my own mistakes—that my fears had heavily engulfed me. We were both fearful and both broken. The time he asked me if we could still see each other but also see other people, I froze. I didn't want that. I didn't think I could handle that. I didn't have strength. I knew I didn't, but maybe I could have. Imagine the growth for me, to be able to release expectations and trust that something beautiful could emerge from that situation. *What if.* Retrospect, hindsight—it's so easy to look back and say what I should have done. Many things, but it's done now.

Almost every single time so far on this trip, things had turned out differently than I had imagined. I knew this applied to many aspects of my life, these expectations. I expected certain things from people, and I created complete, detailed, and precise visions in my mind of how things would happen. Entire conversations. Before I met a met man, I would think about what I would ask him and what I would I say in response to his questions. Not just vague answers. I would think everything through in my mind and imagine myself speaking the words, gesturing with my hands, smiling, and pausing at the right time. It was a script I prepared, that I planned to follow. Sometimes I didn't follow it, but at least I was prepared. Prepared for what? I had no idea. I guess not wanting to say the wrong thing. I had said the wrong things too many times before.

Is it bad to fantasize and create an imaginary world for yourself? Isn't that what manifesting is about? Perhaps I wasn't manifesting at all. I didn't understand what any of that meant. *Why did I do this?* Was I trying to manifest things into my reality, or was I simply making sure I was "prepared" so I wouldn't say anything stupid? Or was I creating a scenario to create a mood? Or was it because I simply wanted to be in control, to make sure I was protected, that I was safe? I guessed it was the last one. But that one bothered me the most. It made me appear off-balance and scared. This wasn't the persona I wanted to project into the world, even if was part of the real me. I was trying to control everything, even the future, and I wanted to show the world that I was balanced and in control when in reality, I was trapped in my own mind most of the time, and my emotions were a wild ride on a roller coaster without end.

As my GPS took me closer to the little cottage I had rented on a horse farm, I realized I was next to a highway. Not just a main road near the little town, but a high-speed, four-lane road. It was another lesson learned. I needed to start asking more questions before I booked on Airbnb. The place was quaint from the outside, and the setting, facing away from the highway, was picturesque. There were several horses in a field and an old barn nearby. I decided it would be just fine for a short stay, and I would go into Memphis tomorrow to see Graceland on my way to my next stop. Maybe even tonight. Although I was tired, I wanted to experience the Memphis blues clubs.

I saw my host near the barn, so I approached her to say hello and get some local info. Although Memphis was about one hour away, I thought I could easily go there that evening. Tired or not, I wanted to explore.

"Hello," I waved and walked over to the tall woman tending to horse-related things.

"Hi. I'm Carol," she said.

She reached out to shake my hand and I shrank back, afraid of getting too close for fear of getting Covid.

"Sorry, I'll keep my distance, if that's okay," I said.

Although I was less fearful in general, I was still afraid of getting sick. What would it matter? I was dying. I wasn't afraid of death. But I wanted a little more time and to die on my terms. Getting sick would interfere with my plans.

"I've been traveling and not sure if I'm contagious or not," I continued.

A half-truth. I was afraid of getting Covid more than I was of passing it on. It was a valid excuse, though.

Carol replied, "It's okay. I've been vaccinated, and I'm comfortable."

I didn't shake her hand, but I smiled.

"I love your farm. It's beautiful," I said.

"Thank you. Do you need anything for the cottage?" she asked.

I didn't bother complaining about the location. It was still beautiful, regardless.

"I think I'm good, thank you. I did want to ask you a question. I'm thinking about going into Memphis to maybe check out a blues place. Do you have any suggestions?"

She looked at me and shook her head.

"You don't want to go by yourself. It's not in the safest area, especially for a woman, and especially at night," she replied.

I was disappointed. Another vision had been killed.

"Really? Why?" I asked.

"Just a lot of crime. Some of it violent," she answered.

I thought about it. *Should I risk it?* Driving there, parking, walking alone…I could Uber. I was still shaken from my encounter with the trucks and was struggling with the desire to go back home. *Better to be safe.* I decided to wait and go another time.

Instead, I asked her for suggestions for some local BBQ.

I ventured out into the small town. I ordered my food and stopped at the liquor store to buy a small bottle of Tennessee whiskey. Armed with delicious local food and drink, I headed back to my cottage. I sat outside on the back deck overlooking the horse paddocks. Although I wasn't a whiskey fan, I drank it anyway, grimacing with each sip. It was part of the experience, so I forced myself to enjoy it. After a few sips, I was a little tipsy. After that, it was easy to chug the rest. *Lightweight.* I should've eaten first. It went well with the BBQ, and the alcohol filled me with confidence and positivity. I was happy! My fears were gone, and I knew I could continue forward. I could do anything. The magic of alcohol. It was the perfect title for a book: "How to Solve Problems with Alcohol." That would be next on my list. Well, further down the line, since I already had two others in progress.

I planned my next stop as I finished my food, deciding if I should go straight across through northern Texas or cut up through Oklahoma and Kansas. I was headed for Denver and wasn't sure which was the best route. I couldn't find many things I wanted to see along either route and made a split-second, drunken decision to go up through Kansas. I found a little farmhouse in the middle of several cornfields, isolated and charming. Feeling fearless, I booked the farmhouse.

I woke up the next morning with a slight headache. I was hungover from my adventures with whiskey. My Airbnb notifications told me I had booked a place. Then I remembered. Kansas and the cornfields. Alcohol hadn't solved my problems in this case but rather made them worse. *Solitude.* I had done it before, and I knew I could do it again, but the farmhouse was surrounded by many miles of farmland. *Big farm. What if a tornado came through?* I imagined a tornado picking up the farmhouse and whisking me away to Oz. *Nope.* Logically, I knew it was unlikely that a tornado would come through. I looked at the forecast. Clear weather.

I had a tornado phobia. *Add that to the list.* And then thinking of the remoteness of the farmhouse, I was anxious. I regretted drinking the whisky. I regretted booking the place. *What do I do?* I was afraid. *Everything will be okay.* Right. Famous last words for everything risky I had ever done. But I decided to follow through. Because I was afraid, I decided to stay there. I would deal with the fear once I arrived.

GHOST OF GRACELAND

The next morning, I drove on to Memphis and Graceland. I was excited. I had no idea what to expect.
I didn't research anything except for tickets and
times. I was going regardless. It was a place I'd chosen to
visit because of a song, and it was on the way. *I wish I could
always be like this. Just flow.* I liked the feeling of simply
experiencing things as they came and not planning. No
expectations meant zero disappointment. I needed to work
on that. Or maybe it didn't even matter. *Life is now definitely
too short for too much self-improvement. Just flow!*

The parking lot wasn't very crowded, so it was relatively
easy to park. Like always, I carried my backpack full of
valuables with me, the heavy burden I carried because of
my fears.

Elvis! The King of Rock and Roll. Not only had he
impacted my childhood, but he also had a huge impact
on the music world. He was different, a rebel in his way,
incorporating what was considered "black sound" into the
mainstream. He was authentic, not fearful of being different,
of standing out. I admired his fearlessness. He'd changed
the music world forever. I was reminded of John Lennon's
quote about Elvis: "Before Elvis there was nothing. If there
hadn't been Elvis, there wouldn't have been the Beatles."

Shortly after his death, I used to listen to his music, and
I sang Elvis's songs into my hairbrush or whatever substitute

I could find for a microphone. I imagined I was onstage, a famous singer. I was free and could sing along to any of his songs. The real me thought I had a terrible voice, but on my make-believe stage, I had the most amazing voice. When we were finished, Elvis would turn to me and say, "Thank ya, thank ya very much."

I would take a bow and go on to the next act. Sometimes it was The Beatles, the other group in my imaginary singing world. Maybe I liked them more than Elvis. *Sorry, Elvis.* The dreams of a child. I wanted to be a singer, but I believed I had a terrible voice. I had wished my voice would miraculously transform into something beautiful. I prayed for a miracle. It hadn't happened, or I would obviously be a famous singer and probably wouldn't be pining over a man. They would be lining up at my door. I laughed. Crazy thoughts of a crazy woman. It was a wonderful dream, though, one that kept me occupied during boring days of being home with nothing else to do except watch reruns of *Gilligan's Island.*

And now, at Graceland, I was reliving my childhood and getting to see how Elvis had lived during his last few years. The number of tickets sold was limited because of the pandemic, and few people were wandering through the property. I drifted from room to room, hoping Elvis would appear to me with some sort of message. I guess I did have expectations. Strange and mysterious occurrences aren't so surprising to me. I'd had my share and was always open to new experiences, especially those beyond the normal existence most people lead. In the past, I'd believed in everything, even energetic love and soulmates. I'd been naïve and delusional, thinking he would eventually come in like a knight in shining armor and save me. Save me from what? Probably from myself. *Now I know better.* The only person who would save me was me.

I was walking past one of the huge staircases in the house when I saw a flash of light out of the corner of my eye. I looked up toward the balcony and I saw a figure. I couldn't make out the features of the face, but I knew it was a man. He had dark hair and was dressed in what looked like pajamas. The pajamas were strange, but I hoped it was Elvis. I turned to make my way up the stairs when he smiled at me. It was him! I was shocked. I shouldn't have been. It had been so easy for me to accept in the past—in those times of pure faith. My father's words of advice and his silhouette in the kitchen smiling back at me were normal occurrences. Sometimes his voice still echoed in my head. *I can't help you if you're sad.*

I heard music and instantly recognized the song. "Can't Help Falling in Love" was playing. Elvis' ghost started singing. For a moment, I thought maybe I was just imagining everything, or maybe this was part of the tour. A sing-along with an Elvis impersonator. But, in the next moment, he flew off the balcony and came toward me. Impersonators don't fly.

I was a little nervous at that point. While I had seen things, they'd been brief and shadowy. This was a crystal clear, full-blown ghost, singing as he floated downstairs. As the music continued, he came to a dead stop in front of me. He then handed me a microphone and said,

"Sing, baby."

I looked around, but nobody was paying attention. Could they see him? Would they be able to hear me? I wanted to sing. *Who cares what anyone thinks!* So I sang.

"Wise men say, only fools rush in…"

"Take my hand…"

Elvis took my hand and started singing along.

I continued. I knew all the lyrics. As I started to sing "some things are meant to be," I was suddenly overcome by sadness. Nothing was meant to be. I stopped singing and handed him back the microphone.

"It's okay. Everything will be okay," he said, reassuring me.

He kissed my cheek, and I then felt him pass right through me. It was like an energetic breeze. Not cold or hot, just a stream of perfect warmth. I think the closest word to describe it was a vibration, a slight murmur of sound and electricity. I turned around, expecting to see him behind me, but there was nothing. He was gone.

He didn't return throughout the rest of my visit. But I carried the memory for the rest of my trip. I wondered what he meant by saying *everything would be okay*. How did he know that? Those were my words. My firm belief was that everything would always be okay. This wasn't a random ghostly appearance. There was a message. Elvis, the ghostly traveler who'd influenced my childhood, had appeared during my visit to tell me *everything would be okay*. Finally, an experience I could relate to and under-stand. There was a purpose to this visit. Although I didn't quite understand how everything would be okay. Another mystery to be solved.

I left, feeling brighter and more positive about the rest of my trip. I didn't feel so alone.

ON THE ROAD AGAIN

It was a long day of driving. What kept me alert was my desperation to get to the mountains of Colorado. I probably could've done the drive in one day. No, it would have been dark. I tried to talk myself into continuing to drive and forget my stop in Kansas. I was still a little fearful, thinking about tornados and isolation. But I needed the stop in Kansas. I needed to sleep. I forced myself to look forward to my little farmhouse surrounded by corn fields in the middle of nowhere.

I drove through Arkansas, making a stop for gas. I thought maybe I should stay in a quaint, rustic little cabin in the Ozarks. Forget Kansas. No, I was going to face my fears.

As I pulled up to the pump, there were a few pickup trucks in the parking lot. There was a little country store called Country Store. *Charming*, I thought to myself. I filled my tank, put on my mask, and made my way inside to use the bathroom and buy more snacks (I believed in stocking up wherever I stopped). I pushed the door and walked in. Every single male head turned toward the door. None were wearing masks. None were smiling. I wish they had been wearing masks, at least I could have pretended they were smiling. *These are not friendly faces*, I thought. None of them were the men of my dreams. I'm sure they saw me as an outsider. I took a deep breath and cleared my head. I wasn't going to judge anyone or anything.

"What do you need?" asked a gravelly voice.

I turned my head to reply and saw the men. Four, maybe five, sitting around the counter. Were they drinking? *I'm dead.*

"May I use the bathroom? I asked, in a meek, polite voice.

May I use the bathroom? Now they definitely know I'm not from around here. Way to make myself stick out. The last thing I wanted to do was be different.

An older man looked me over, up and down, his eyes pausing at my face, and pointed to the back. *All right.* I grasped my phone in my hand in case I needed to dial 911 and walked quickly toward the rear of the store. I wanted to hurry and get out of there as fast as I could. I could have just found another bathroom. *Or just peed my pants.* I couldn't wait. It was dark back there, but I found a door. Scrawled in red Sharpie was what looked like the word, *Ladies.* It was haphazardly written, almost illegible. It was either written by a five-year-old or a serial killer. I looked for another door, one that would say, *Gentlemen,* just to be sure I wasn't reading incorrectly. But the only other door I found simply said, *M* in black Sharpie. *Well, I guess that's for the men.* I chose door number one with the creepy, red writing, praying that it didn't lead to a secret room where I would be bound and gagged and held prisoner for months. I paused for a second as I lightly touched the doorknob, looking around to make sure nobody was hiding in the dark corners near the bathroom area.

I used the bathroom as fast as I could, didn't wash my hands, *no soap and no time,* and rushed out. No snacks. I would survive.

"Thank you," I called out as I ran past the men. I felt their eyes follow me as I left the *Country Store.* I sprinted to my car, slammed the door shut, and locked myself in, safe again. I Purelled my hands. *Purelled is now a verb in everyone's vocabulary.* I started the car, vowing never to return to the *Country Store* again. I was alone. I was a woman. I was an outsider. I was afraid. *It was ridiculous.* They'd done nothing to cause concern.

I had imagined myself casually chatting with the local people in the charming country store. Buying some homemade goods, hearing about their real lives. Connecting to people and breaking the walls of division. That hadn't happened because I'd been afraid and had made an impulsive judgment. They were different, they were men, I was alone, and therefore they were dangerous. I still had some fears to deal with. *I should probably make a list of my fears.*

Suddenly, there was a tap on my window. I was startled and screamed. It was one of the men, and he was smiling. He held up a credit card. Mine. It must have fallen out of my pocket.

"Ma'am, you dropped this. You ran out so fast, I tried to tell you," he said.

I opened my window. I can't believe the thoughts that had gone through my mind in that store. Expectations again, but this time, the bad turned into the good. He had kind eyes and there was nothing sinister.

"Thank you so much," I said as I took the card from him.

"And here, this is for you," he replied, handing me a jar of homemade blueberry jam.

I nearly cried. I was so touched by his action, despite my obvious fear of being in the store. I knew, being a woman traveling alone, I'd been nervous. I loved being surprised by this random act of kindness. It gave me faith in humanity. And in myself.

I HAVE A FEELING WE'RE NOT IN KANSAS… BUT WAIT…

I drove through Oklahoma, via Tulsa. I got sandwiched between two trucks again and the anxiety crept in. I needed to escape. This time, I was close to the front of the trucks and decided to speed past them. When I was finally in the clear, I saw blue and red lights behind me. *Shit.* The last thing I wanted was a ticket. I pulled over, wondering how fast I was going. I knew I wasn't going any faster than any of the other cars around me. Out-of-state plates and slightly tinted windows—I stood out. I hoped the trooper would be kind. *Should I cry?* No, I didn't think that would work. I'd tried that once before and the officer had been cold and had given me a ticket anyway.

When I rolled down the window, he seemed surprised to see me. Had he expected someone else? I gave him my license and opened the glove compartment, telling him I needed to open it to get my registration. When I pulled it open, my pepper spray fell out, still in its original packaging.

"Oh, someone gave this to me, in case I needed to protect myself. I'm traveling alone and…" I babbled for a solid minute, explaining myself, worried that pepper spray was illegal and I would be arrested.

He took my license and registration and said, "Ma'am, it doesn't do you any good in the package."

I was momentarily relieved. I told him the story of the trucks and how I always obeyed the law and hardly ever sped. More babbling. He didn't seem as if he was paying attention. *Please, please. No ticket.* Thankfully, he only gave me a warning and told me to slow down and be careful. And he reminded me to open my pepper spray. It was a sobering experience after Graceland, but it didn't faze me. Except I did slow down—for a few hours, at least.

I drove straight up through Kansas to a little town just south of Wichita. I looked forward to seeing the quaint town and what it had to offer. Really, by now I should've known. The little town was far from a quaint Kansas village, with few local stores and shops. It was full of fast-food places and strip malls. When I asked my host where to find dinner, she gave me suggestions for Taco Bell and Wendy's. Was it Sunday again and everything was closed? Couldn't be. *Sigh.* I opted to go to the grocery store instead and cook something healthy for myself. I added a bottle of wine to my cart. *I would probably need it tonight.*

The farmhouse was charming on the outside, but was a bit run down and frumpy on the inside. *Don't judge a book by its cover. Beauty is on the inside.* No, those did not apply. There were dust bunnies in the corner, a thick layer of dirt and grime on the baseboards, and someone's leftover crusty food in the microwave. The furniture looked like it was from the 1950s and had seen better days. It was gloomy, dark, and creepy. *Haunted*? I felt a chill. I wanted to leave, but I had no place to go. I was tired and decided to ignore the dirt and the bad energy and just enjoy the peace. It was peaceful. Quiet. Remote. And when the sun set, it was pitch dark outside. I was able to see the full night sky filled with millions of shining stars.

I thought about how I was just a tiny particle in a vast universe. Part of something larger that maybe one day I would comprehend. *Or part of nothing at all except my imagination.* I was insignificant. We all are. Small particles of energy in the vastness of the universe. It was awesome and intimidating at the same time.

These moments of quiet, peaceful reflection were rare for me during that time. My insignificance didn't bother me. It made me feel as if I was a part of something larger. It gave me some comfort. Although I was less scared than on the previous nights, I still thought about the what-ifs. Worry and hope, bound together trying to predict the future.

The old farmhouse was two stories and was probably built in the 1800s, if not earlier. Upstairs, the floors were slanted, as if the house was about to fall over on its side. It was a little disconcerting. I was worried it would collapse with my weight, so I decided to sleep in the bedroom on the ground floor. It was closer to the front door anyway, in case I needed to make a quick escape. I didn't shower. I smelled, but I kept thinking about *Psycho*, and that someone would stab me to death. I ate a quick dinner of veggies and rice and locked myself in my bedroom, leaving the lights on. I realized locking my room was probably pointless, but it made me feel better. Like leaving the lights on everywhere. *At least I would be able to see what was coming toward me.*

What if something happened? What if I needed medical care? What if someone came to kill me? What if it's haunted? I couldn't sleep. Although I thought I was calm and less fearful, when I lay in bed, I realized I was still overly anxious. I watched something on Netflix for a few hours, something mindless and boring, until I finally fell asleep from exhaustion.

A giant thud at four a.m. startled me. I knew I wasn't dreaming. I heard a loud noise, and it sounded like it had come from upstairs. Then I heard it again. *Shit.* A ghost? I didn't want to inspect where it had come from. I just wanted to ignore it. I calmly got out of bed, phone in hand. I thought about my pepper spray that I'd foolishly left in my glove compartment. Again. *Damn.* I didn't think I would need it—*What use was pepper spray against a ghost?* Too late anyway. I grabbed a lamp and just stood there, contemplating what to do. *Should I go upstairs?* I decided no. Maybe it was all in my mind.

I waited for the banging sound to return. It didn't. I talked myself into believing that I had been dreaming and opened the door. There was no way I could go back to sleep. I drank my coffee, packed my things, planned my route, and left. Despite my abrupt departure, I saw it as a victory. I made it through the night, in complete isolation, with at least some sleep. I was alive. And maybe a little less fearful than I had been during my first night on the road.

As I backed out of the driveway, I saw movement in an upstairs window of the farmhouse. I looked up at the window and saw a figure. No, it was more like a long beam of light swaying back and forth. I had no idea what it was. I wanted to go back into the house because I felt an overwhelming sensation of love and positive energy coming from the light. But the scared part of me backed out of the driveway and went onward to Denver. Something or someone was trying to send me a message. Maybe I should've stayed.

No, I had to keep moving. It was all in my head. I didn't know what was real anymore. If there was anything to understand, I would eventually find the answer. *Hopefully.* I still had many unanswered questions.

I drove down the long and bumpy gravel road. I was on the road, ready to get to where I was going. But then I had to stop and wait for a very long freight train to pass at the railroad crossing. I was the only car on the road. I listened to the sound of the wheels on the rails, a rhythmic sound that almost put me to sleep. I was tired after very little sleep. I waited. Nearly twenty minutes later, the train finally passed, and I was on my way.

PENNIES FROM HEAVEN

I realized I needed more coffee. And a picture of the beautiful sunrise. As I prepared to pull off the highway to the nearest open coffee shop, I saw a yellow plane flying low, parallel to the highway. I watched it suddenly turn right toward the highway, losing altitude. It was coming right toward me. I quickly pulled over to the shoulder and got out of my car, waiting to see what would happen next. I felt the wind as the plane swooped down, maybe ten feet above my head. Too close. The plane then flew up, almost vertically, and then did a loop de loop and headed back toward me. *What the hell is this person doing?* He—he was a *he* in my mind—was either drunk or suicidal. I waved my arms, hoping he would see me. He kept coming. I ran into the woods on the side of the road. He continued on his path, again flying about ten feet over my head. Something fell out of the plane. Or from the sky. It was hard to tell. He then flew back to where he had come from and disappeared.

When I knew I was safe, I went to see what had fallen. I reached down. There was a small box. I picked it up and inside found a golden coin. It had writing on both sides and a picture of a hawk. *My spirit animal.* The words on one side of the coin said, *What you seek*, and on the other, *is already here*. I didn't know what that meant. *What's the message, what's the meaning? What I seek*—I didn't know what I was seeking. The connectivity of the answers to some meaningful questions? The perfect man? Love? I was seeking so many things at once. But which one was already here?

I kept a lookout for the airplane after I got my coffee, but I didn't see it again. I put the coin in my pocket and continued on my way.

BOREDOM

At first, I found the Kansas countryside beautiful. The flat areas and the surrounding farms still had some color, and occasionally, I could see a few rolling hills. I didn't understand how people could say driving through Kansas was boring.

However, after a few hours, the scenery was no longer as beautiful. It was repetitive, with endless fields and farms. I wanted nothing but to see mountains. The biggest thrill from my drive was the tumbleweeds. It was a windy day, enough to make my car occasionally shift from side to side, and several gigantic tumbleweeds crossed my path. I had never seen a tumbleweed. Maybe. I couldn't remember if I had at one point when I was younger, but to me, this was a first. Giant tumbleweeds in Kansas while driving solo cross country. That was new for me. *My first and last tumbleweeds before I die.*

I couldn't wait to get to the Colorado border. I expected a change in scenery. However, that didn't happen. It was the same, flat, boring scenery. I expected the landscape to change, but I had forgotten that the Rockies were still far away. More boring landscape.

I was tired. And bored. And my mind began to wander. Meandering back to the past, love, men, loss. Analyzing every experience I'd ever had with a man. From my first love to my last. My vivid memories, the unforgettable details that had kept me tied to things that were dead and gone. I appreciated that I could remember the details. I could honestly say, "You once told me…" This was both a wonderful thing and a terrible thing. Wonderful to remember beautiful memories. And terrible to remember those things that hurt us that we want to forget. Maybe everyone is like this. Maybe everyone remembers but they choose to forget, to let things go, let go of the pain that no longer matters, and the joy that can never be attained. My problem was everything was so clear it was hard to forget.

I wished I could forget him. I used to wake up some days and jokingly beg the Universe to erase the memories, obliterate the sadness, even the joy. The happy moments were worse. To feel the feelings, to know them, deeply, was to want them again. Knowing you can't have that moment back, and it is only a memory, makes it so much worse. I had felt so stuck after the end of things. I only had one choice—move on and forget—and that's what I tried to do by filling my life with men. I didn't sleep around. I didn't do hookups, and I chose very carefully whom I slept with. It wasn't many. Only the ones I deemed "worthy." *Worthy of what? Of me? Of my energy?* I wasn't giving myself away to just anyone. I believed I made careful choices, meticulously sorting through the pros and cons and sensing what type of people they were.

It appears I made very poor choices. It took me a long time to realize I was choosing the *wrong* men. I chose them. They did not fall into my life as gifts from the Universe, as I had assumed. In the end, they were either emotionally unavailable, fearful of commitment, or just after sex. I mean, I enjoyed the sex. Some of them were great lovers. But I wanted more, and it seemed as if they wanted less. I was getting old, and the older I got, the more my looks faded. More gray, more wrinkles. Who would want me when I was old and wrinkly? How would I ever find a companion then?

Why did I even want a companion so desperately? Loneliness? I wasn't lonely. I loved spending time on my own. Desperation. Fear. Fear of being alone later. Dying alone. Not having anyone to share those quiet moments of life, coffee by the river, walking in the woods. Would I always be alone? I wasn't made to be single. *Made? Made by who?* Why did I choose this life? Why did I choose to live a life alone when I wanted so badly to be with someone? And what did it even matter?

I would be gone soon. Alone or not, I would be gone.

CHECK ENGINE

Then something terrible happened. As I was driving along pondering my loneliness and mortality, I heard a loud and horrible grinding noise. *Shit*. The "check engine" light came on and the car abruptly stopped its forward movement. I panicked for a moment, losing control of the car. I swerved to the left, then to the right. White-knuckling the steering wheel, I struggled to control the movement of the car. After a few seconds, I finally regained control and slowly rolled to the shoulder.

I quickly put the car into park and pushed the off button, although it seemed to me the car was already off. I tried to restart it. It wouldn't start. The "check engine" light likely meant a catastrophic failure. *God, I hope I have cell service.* Thankfully I did. I called AAA and they said they would have someone out as soon as possible. About two to three hours, in my case. I was pretty much in the middle of nowhere, somewhere in Kansas-like Colorado.

As I waited, I pulled the coin from my pocket, thinking maybe I had missed something. I read the words *What you seek* and flipped the coin over. To my surprise, the words were different. Instead of, *is already here*, the coin now said, *is in your heart.*

My heart? My heart screwed things up for me. Why would I want to look at my heart? My heart was the problem, not the answer. If this was a message from the Universe, it made little sense. I had already agreed with the Universe that my problems stemmed from my heart. My heart messed up my intuition. They were not connected. Intuition is clear and unemotional. But I had to do something with that message. *Not now. Later.* I put the coin away.

AAA came and towed my car to the nearest repair station. They said it was best to get things checked out. The strangest thing was that my car checked out fine at the station. It started immediately. The man, Kenny, said the transmission may be going but it was hard to say when. Could be anything, but there was nothing they could do without finding a problem. *Damn.* I wanted to keep going. I wasn't finished with my adventure yet. "*Do I risk it? Do I keep driving west?*" I asked Kenny. He cautioned against it and said I could try replacing the transmission or maybe even buy a new car. My car had almost 200,000 miles and would cost too much money to repair. It seemed crazy. And I certainly didn't want to buy a new car on the road. I decided to keep going. Worst case, if my car died, I would buy a new one. Or fix it. It didn't matter to me. I wasn't afraid. Normally I would have been in panic mode, calling someone for help or figuring out some way to get home. I felt confident everything would be just fine as I got back in my car and continued driving west, singing "Rocky Mountain High" as I drove past a multitude of tumbleweeds and flat fields.

FREEDOM

I was ecstatic to finally see the mountains. At first, they were small and out of focus. Too far and blurry for me to see all the details without my glasses on. I never wore them, except when it was dark or maybe stormy. I didn't want to become dependent, I told myself, year after year, as my vision slowly grew fuzzier. I refused. I only used them when I had to, driving in the dark, so the world would be a bit clearer. I wasn't blind. I could see things. I just couldn't read things. Except for shadows or spirits, of course. Those I could always see, with or without glasses.

The closer I got to the mountains, the freer I felt. The heaviness I had carried through Kansas and the other flat states sloughed off as if slowly melting in the sun, lifting off a layer of dark to reveal the light underneath. *I will climb those mountains. I'm not stopping until I reach the top.* I was determined. *Please, please, Universe, let my car make it!*

I made it past Denver and continued west. I stopped for a few pictures, the huge expanse of mountains stretching across the horizon. I'd seen mountains before, but this was a new mountain range, full of new possibilities. I had never been to Colorado, never been to the Rockies. *Maybe I had driven through the northern Rockies.* Somewhere in my mind, I kept remembering things that may or may not have been true. Like the tumbleweeds. A vague memory of a quick pass through the Rockies, not even stopping for a picture. Very strange. *I've been here before*—I was sure of it. Maybe in a dream. Or a past life. So many moments that seemed to intersect and connect.

What if I was living in a dream? What if my reality was something different? Better or worse? It must be worse, or I would wake myself up already. Maybe I couldn't wake up. I wanted to know. Was I sleeping, and all of this was created by me? If so, why wouldn't I have already found my dream man? I could easily create him, right? Or was I in someone else's dream? That was even more fascinating. Who exactly was dreaming about me, and why was I stuck? All I know is that if I were living in a dream, I'd want to know so that I could change the dream. I'd also want to know what the waking state was like before I woke up. I would hate to wake up to something worse.

I once had a dream within a dream. The dream started with an old boyfriend from many years ago. I hadn't thought about him in a long time and usually, when I did, it was with a little regret. I tried hard not to deeply regret the past, so the regret was small, at least compared to my worries about the future. I had loved him, but I'd let him go. I never understood why until later. It was just after college graduation, and we had spent most of the summer together. I had no plans, and I was anxious about my future.

The dream played out exactly like it had in real life. Maybe. I'm not one hundred percent sure because the exact details of the actual event escape me. Usually, I remember everything, but those memories were foggy.

He turned to me and said, "Let's just go. Go west, go to California, get jobs, find a place to live and start a new life."

I laughed.

"I'm not kidding," he replied.

He was serious. There was no plan, no security. He was as poor as I was, both of us with nothing (or less than nothing, since I was in credit card debt hell back then). I loved him. But I was too scared of the uncertainty.

"No, I can't. I'm not ready," I said.

He mumbled something, and I mumbled something back. In the dream, we stood facing each other, saying incomprehensible words.

I have no idea what was said in both the dream and real life. No clue. I can't remember what reason I gave him or what made him leave without me. I can't remember, and I'm still not sure why.

All I remember is that he got in his car and drove away as I watched from my window. I was sad. Not deeply sad or in terrible pain. I was relieved. *Strange.* I loved him. Yet I was okay with him going.

One second later, there was a knock on my door (it was about twenty minutes in real life). *Who is that?* I wondered. I knew who it was. But my dream self must have been confused.

I opened the door, and there he stood with a simple but beautiful bouquet from the local grocery store.

"Come with me," he begged.

"I can't…" I shook my head and looked down.

He handed me the flowers, kissed me, and walked away. He said something else, something else I can't remember, and I watched him drive away, a mixture of sadness and relief.

I was surprised to see him in my dream. I hadn't thought about him for a long time, and when I did, it was with a tinge of regret. I should have gone with him. I'd loved him.

I wished I had chosen differently. Perhaps the path of my life would've been entirely altered. Was that a good thing to have an entirely different life? Sometimes I would say yes. But I still felt strongly that everything that I'd experienced had brought me to this exact moment in time. In the happy moments, I was grateful for my choices.

Then everything shifted in the dream, and he was there again, but we were in a different place. He put his arms around me and said he loved me. I told him, "*I know, but what do you have to offer me besides love?*" A very strange thing to say. Isn't love enough? He replied, "O*nly love.*" He would give me love. In my dream, I accepted the love. I didn't need anything else. Then I noticed someone was right above me, just barely in my scope of vision—a shadow puppet master, and he was controlling my dream. He manipulated my dream, and I was suddenly in another dream, a dream within a dream. In this dream within a dream, I was still sleeping. I was dreaming that I was dreaming about my old boyfriend.

He released me, his arms slowly floating out of my view, and again the dream shifted. I saw a giant walking toward me. I could feel the vibrations from his heavy steps. It was the giant from my childhood nightmares. He'd often appeared when I was a child, and I was always running from him, hiding whenever and wherever I could. The dreams continued into adulthood, although not as often. I finally banished him by not running. Instead, I defiantly stood my ground as he moved toward me. He looked at me, shrugged, and walked away. I never saw him again.

Why had he returned? I had to wake up. I tried to wake up. I saw myself asleep and I yelled to myself to wake up. My dream self tried but was frozen, stuck in some other place.

"Wake up!" I screamed.

My sleeping dream-self opened her eyes. Panic. All I could see was panic in my eyes. I couldn't move, and I couldn't wake up. I'd be stuck like this forever. I grabbed sleeping me's arm and scratched it with a nail I found on the ground. Sleeping me screamed and abruptly woke up. But I wasn't awake yet. Sleeping me was still in a dream, and the giant was coming. I wasn't even sure how to get through the other layer and wake up. I just willed it. I woke myself up. The fog lifted as I returned to the waking world. I was panting and tears streamed down my face, a long bleeding scratch on my arm. I felt a deep sadness I'd never experienced about the love I let go. I never thought to mourn him. I had never perceived him as a deep loss. *What was lost was by my own choice.* Love wasn't enough back then. I wanted security, too. Perhaps only security was enough. *Fool.*

HIGHER AND HIGHER

I headed toward the mountains, higher, up toward Aspen, not even sure how I was still going. I was tired and had been driving all day. I was worried about my car, but I felt everything would be okay. I always felt everything would be okay when I was balanced. If my emotions overwhelmed me, especially with worry, I lost all sense of positivity. What if everything went wrong (what is everything, anyway)? What if *I* was wrong? What if I was not as intuitive as I thought I was? What if I was simply unrealistic, full of toxic positivity? Then the worry crept in like a choking vine, climbing and overtaking me, making me feel trapped and unable to control anything in my life. Most of the time, it doesn't last too long. I'm usually able to cut away the vine, eventually. *I wish it wouldn't grow back.* I would love to just pull the roots completely from the ground so the plant could no longer entangle me. Is that even possible? It seems unrealistic. Sometimes a bit of worry might be good. Especially when you have a car that needs repairs and may not make it over the next hill.

I did make it. I found a cabin for the night (or maybe two, I hadn't decided) just outside Aspen. I had a friend there and hoped we could get together.

The biggest problem for me was the altitude. I had forgotten about the possibility of altitude sickness in the mountains. I was out of breath and tired with a slight headache, and by the time I finished unloading my numerous boxes and bags, I felt like I was getting sick. Not a great feeling.

Although it was another secluded cabin, I slept deeply that night for the first time since I'd started my trip. Alone, but finally relaxed. I knew I would never again be afraid of being alone, at least physically.

I still didn't feel great when I woke up, still a little head-achy but determined to explore. I left my cabin and headed toward the nearest hiking path.

Being alone and hiking in the mountains, I only felt a little anxiety, mostly about being mauled by bears. It was quiet and very remote, and I didn't have cell service. My only connection to the outside world was the Wi-Fi in the cabin, so I was on my own trekking through the wilderness. In reality, it was not a very wise decision to go off alone and not let anyone know where I was. But I wanted to get over my fear, and I knew the only way to evolve was to confront what I feared. *I would be okay*. I knew it. At least, *in the end*, everything would be okay. I was not even sure what that meant when I thought about it. *In the end* should have put me in a more vigilant mode.

I was slowly strolling on a small path between several majestic mountain peaks, taking my time and not in a rush to get anywhere. I was awed by the beauty. I sat on a rock, having a small snack and some water. A perfect place for a picnic.

That's when I heard a rustling sound to my left. I quickly turned and saw a brownish-black shadow. *I hope that it's just a shadow or a ghost.*

It wasn't. It was a bear.

A very large black bear. I heard there were no brown bears in the Rockies. Brown bears are easier to escape from and are not as aggressive as black bears. *Shit.* I didn't have bear spray and I didn't have a plan. I was just flowing along in my toxic positivity, believing everything was going to be okay. I had to think everything was going to be okay at that point. I had to act like everything was okay, or the bear would sense my fear and come after me. *I think I'm supposed to freeze and crouch.* I didn't remember. I crouched. The bear inched closer and then stopped, looking at me with curiosity. *Or hunger.* I could see his eyes. They looked human. It had seen me or smelled me or both. He knew I was there. I stopped myself from looking at him. I knew I shouldn't look him in the eye. I could sense him observing me, deciding if I was an enemy, deciding whether to walk away or attack.

I tried to stay calm, even though I was terrified. *Black bears are aggressive. Wait, maybe that was brown bears?* I couldn't remember. I had nothing to protect myself. I couldn't remember what to do. I prayed. For my life. For the bear to go away. I wanted to run, but took control of myself, knowing it was better to be still.

Then it charged. It was rushing right toward me, and it was bigger than I thought. A huge, angry bear. Could it be a grizzly? I didn't even think grizzlies came this far south. I didn't know what kind of bear it was. All I knew is that it was that he was furious.

I crouched, crying silently in fear. I wanted to close my eyes but thought it best to keep them open. My memory isn't clear. I don't remember what else I did—I could have peed my pants for all I knew.

I heard a hissing sound and a man's voice.

"Run to the right, down the path!" said the voice.

I didn't look to see who it was, nor did I hesitate. I ran. I sprinted away as fast as I could down the path. Everything was a blur, and I didn't stop until I heard the same male voice telling me to stop.

"It's okay. It's gone. You can stop running now."

I saw the stranger just behind me. He was beautiful. I know that's not usually the word people would use to describe a man, especially a presumptively rugged man who just happened to save me from a bear. But he was beautiful. Ethereal. Luminous. He had a full beard and long hair and was only wearing a t-shirt and jeans. No shoes, despite the coolness of the day. *Was he real?*

"OMG…Thank…you," I told him, completely out of breath.

I couldn't believe I had said "OMG." As if I was texting. *LOL*, I thought to myself.

Then darkness.

MOUNTAIN MAN

s I slowly opened my eyes, I realized I was indoors in an unfamiliar place. It was dark outside. I could see a fire in the old stone fireplace, and I was covered by several thick blankets. I still wore my long-sleeved t-shirt and my pants. I wasn't sure where the rest of my clothes were. As my eyes adjusted, I saw that it was a small, sparsely decorated cabin. Simple but cozy. I sat up and looked around. No other people. I was alone, unsure how I got there.

I wasn't sure whether to be afraid. *Funny thing to think.* Fear usually exists or it doesn't. You feel it or you don't. I should've been afraid, waking up in a strange place after blacking out somewhere in the mountains. I remembered the mountain man and how he had saved me from the bear. *Am I in his man cave?* I could see the headline: *Woman Disappears in Colorado Mountains.* I thought it was better for me to get up and just leave.

I looked for the rest of my clothes. Then the door opened and in walked the mountain man, the hero or serial killer who had saved me from the bear. I should've been scared, waking up in a strange cabin with a man I didn't know. Strangely, I wasn't. When I looked at him, I immediately trusted him. I knew him from somewhere. *How could I know him?*

It was a knowing. I had met this man before, either in this life or a previous life. Or maybe in my dreams. I used to dream of a man. For many years, since childhood, out of nowhere, I would dream of him. I loved him and he loved me. The dream was infused with a comforting feeling of love. Of home. The dream disappeared once I met *him*, the man I'd thought was the love of my life, the one I'd thought was meant for me. I'd believed he was the same man from my dreams. But everything had fallen apart between us. *I don't know, anymore, if he is the same man.* The dreams had stopped, but we weren't together. I didn't know what it meant, but the feeling of love had gone from both my sleeping world and my real life. The man before me emitted that same warmth and comfort. I presumed I was safe, which defied all logic. *I fear at the wrong times.*

"You're awake," he said, as he placed more wood on the fire.

He was still wearing only a t-shirt and jeans and was still barefoot. The cold didn't seem to bother him.

"Yes," I replied. "Where am I?"

"My home," he answered.

Home. It felt like home. *I shouldn't feel safe. He could still be a serial killer.* But even as I searched for reasons to heighten my fear, my intuition told me there was nothing to fear. I had to trust that feeling. I had no choice. I was already trapped in a cabin with a strange man.

Everything will be okay.

He walked over to me and handed me a mug.

"Here, have some tea."

Tea? Or poison? My mind was still trying to step in the way. *Or was that my heart?* I didn't know anymore.

I took a sip.

"Thank you."

I had to get back to my cabin. But I also wanted to stay. I felt safe there, protected. I needed answers.

I stood up, took one of the blankets from the bed with me, and moved to the couch.

"What happened?" I asked.

He told me how after he scared the bear away, I fainted, and he brought me here. A simple story with no details.

Fainted? It must have been the altitude. I'm not a fainter. I usually just cry in stressful situations.

"Oh." I turned my body and sat up straight on the couch. "I need to get home."

He looked straight into my eyes. I could feel him reading me, looking right into my soul, my heart. That was disconcerting.

"Well," he said, sitting next to me, "it's dark and snowing. You'll have to wait until morning."

I could feel the warm energy of his body. He was just a few inches from me. I didn't want to wait until morning, despite the warmth and comfort of the cabin. And the warmth of his body. He seemed harmless.

What if my intuition is wrong?

"Can you drive me?" I asked.

As comfortable as I felt, I knew I should probably get back to my cabin.

He laughed. "No, I don't have a car."

Who doesn't have a car?

I wondered how he got groceries or other supplies. He probably lived off the land. It could be done. Did he have a bathroom? I needed to use the bathroom.

"The bathroom is right back there," he replied, pointing away from the front door, reading my thoughts.

I quickly used the bathroom. It too was cozy and simple. He had running water, which meant some sort of plumbing system. I wanted to take a shower. I smelled. Maybe. I decided to wait. I walked back toward him. I had no choice but to stay unless I wanted to hike alone in the cold, dark night. *Nope. I couldn't.* I had to trust him.

The rest of the night was a blur. We talked for a long time, sharing stories. I learned that he had been living up here off the grid for several years. He was self-sufficient. A real mountain man. He also wrote, but just for himself. I asked him what types of stories and he answered, whatever Spirit conveys. He was a spiritual mountain man. I was irresistibly pulled toward him, energetically. I felt our separate energies align and then combine. We were intertwined.

As we talked, our bodies moved closer to each other. I remember kissing him and he kissed me back. I woke up later that night, lying in his arms.

SHAPESHIFTING

He was still sleeping. I stared at him for a long time, looking over his beautiful, rugged, and very sincere face. I could read him easily as he slept. He was so at peace, the same peace I desired. Confident, strong, fearless. *He's my mountain man.*

The memories came back. We'd had incredible sex. No, it was more than that. It was transcendental, a deeply connected experience. It was beyond the physical.

I realized I didn't even know his name. Did he know mine? I'd slept with a man who had saved my life and brought me to a remote cabin somewhere in the Rockies. The bear man.

Maybe it was time to go.

No, I told my fear, *you can trust him.*

I closed my eyes, feeling his warmth, and thought I would go back to sleep. Then I felt a sudden rush of heat. I opened my eyes and looked at him. He was a bear. He was *the* bear that had chased me. His eyes fluttered open—those human eyes I had seen on the trail. I wondered if I was dreaming, but it was too clear to be a dream. Fearlessly, I reached out to touch his face. I closed my eyes. As I touched him, I felt a human face, the scruffiness of his beard, his neck, down to his muscular shoulders and arms. The bear was gone. I kept going, sliding my hand down his torso. He was so warm, fiery. I pulled myself closer to him.

He turned me over, my back toward him, and wrapped his arms around me. I opened my eyes and swiveled my head to look at him. He was no longer a bear, but the man who had saved my life. I felt safe. Comfortable. *Home.* I was home, and I never wanted to leave. I fell back to sleep warmed in the flame of the bear man.

When I finally woke up, he was gone. I wondered if I had been dreaming, or if he had metamorphosed into a bear. It was possible. Anything was possible. I believed. I was still in a beautiful daze. I didn't want this experience to end. I didn't want to leave. I didn't want him to leave. I panicked for a moment, that he was gone. *Maybe he's outside.*

I couldn't find my clothes, so I wrapped myself in a thick, furry blanket and stepped outside the cabin. He was there, sitting on a log, watching the sunrise, completely naked.

The snow had stopped, and I could see the clear sky, the moon setting in the west and the blanket of stars growing dimmer.

"Good morning," he said, without turning around.

I walked toward him and stood in front of him. I asked him his name. I needed to know that.

He didn't answer but stood up, pulling the blanket apart and enfolding us both beneath the warmth. His body was hot, even though he had been sitting naked in the cold. I wanted to stay there forever.

"What's your name?" I asked again.

"I already told you," he answered.

I didn't recall him telling me his name. Maybe it had been in a moment of uncontrollable passion, when I was in a daze, lost to reality. I felt slightly embarrassed, having forgotten what he'd told me. Memories are quite clear, but names often escape me. *Too many men.*

"Tell me again," I replied, hoping he wasn't aware of my memory lapse.

"Bear," he answered.

I thought he was joking. But he looked completely serious. *I would have remembered him telling me that.*

"Seriously, what's your real name?"

"Does it matter?" he whispered in my ear.

"That's not your real name," I said, laughing. "Tell me."

He looked at me and said, "I am whoever you want me to be."

Can you be my lover? I asked myself.

I heard the reply in my head. *I can be a present lover.*

A telepathic connection. I flowed.

A future lover? I hoped.

Always in the present. I'm here now, he replied.

He kissed me, picked me up, and carried me back to the cabin. We made love. Passionate, fearless, connected, timeless love. I was so happy. *I'm never going back to my old life. I'm going to live forever with my mountain man. Or bear man.* Either name was fine with me. The Mountain Bear man. The Bare Mountain man. I laughed to myself at my joke.

LIFE IS BUT A DREAM

I woke up to darkness. I reached over to touch him but couldn't find him. I sat up. He was gone. As I looked around, I realized I was back in my cabin, in my own bed. And he was gone. I anxiously stood up and went to the door, opening it, hoping to find him outside. He wasn't there. Just the dark. The sun had been rising when I was with him last. I wondered how it could be dark again. Had an entire day passed?

"Where are you?" I yelled into the woods.

No reply. I was cold. I went back inside and quickly got dressed. I would go and find him. The sun would rise soon, and it would be daylight. But it wouldn't have mattered. I would have gone searching for him in the dark.

I returned to the spot where I had first met him, hoping to find the cabin nearby. I wasn't scared anymore of getting lost or encountering bears. I wandered, searching for him and the cabin for a long time. But I never found him.

Maybe it had all been a dream? My intuition told me *no.* It was an unbelievable, amazing experience. Even for me, it seemed unbelievable. A man called Bear. Who had saved my life and provided me with warmth.

Another one of my fantastical dreams? No. *I believe.*

When I returned to my cabin, I learned the truth. On the bed, I found a leather necklace with a hand-carved wooden bear totem pendant. I knew it was from him. And I knew I wouldn't see him again.

Again, a knowing. *I believe.*

A deep sadness swept over me. *I love him.* I would have stayed with him, lived in the mountains, lived off the land. What better way to die than in the arms of a mountain man? *Why do they keep leaving me?* I knew that wasn't true. The leaving was often mutual. That's just my mind, my fear, speaking to me. The mountain man didn't leave me. He just left because he was on a solo journey, like me.

FORGIVENESS

I had felt abandoned by him, my soulmate from the past. He had rejected me and walked away. It took me a long time to realize the truth. I had walked away from him. I'd created a narrative in my mind that I was the victim. But he was as much a victim as I was. I'd hurt him as much as he'd hurt me. I'd been many things—impatient, pushy, and wanting everything from him at once. I hadn't wanted to work at it. I hadn't even given it a chance to work. I'd pushed and pushed, demanding that he love me. It was incomprehensible that he hadn't, and I'd needed it so desperately back then. To be loved in return. And I hated myself for it. For wanting love.

I'd been insecure. Fearful. I'd been just as fearful as he was, but I hadn't even realized that. Had I feared putting in the work? It was confusing, looking back. I had tried so hard to make it work, but we'd never cooperated or collaborated in any way. It had just been me, hopeful and giving all my energy to making the relationship work. Impatiently wanting everything right away and trying to find the quickest way possible to win him over. As I tried to clearly understand my role in everything, I only knew that I carried some of the blame. I'd looked at him, into his eyes and I saw my reflection. We'd mirrored each other and triggered each other and acted impulsively. I'd feared abandonment. I'd feared rejection. I'd tried to force his hand. I'd been as ruthless as the Queen of Hearts.

I realized all this, and I was angry with myself. *But I hadn't known, back then.* I needed to forgive not only him but also myself for the mistakes I'd made. It had been difficult to forgive myself because I'd only blamed him. I hoped that by understanding things, I could now clear the path forward by forgiving myself. I had already forgiven him. I held no anger or judgment. I understood, always, the why and the what. I hoped that this would finally free me from whatever ties still bound me to him. It's difficult to move on without forgiveness.

I felt more at peace, knowing all this.

And now I had to keep going wherever I was going and continue my quest. I put the bear pendant around my neck, packed up my car, and left the mountains. West toward the ocean—that's where I would find more answers. The bear man had shown me that not all was lost. There was still hope for love. Not that it mattered in my lifetime at that moment but understanding that the connectedness was not exclusive to my past love, that it was possible elsewhere, was a welcome release before death.

A GIFT

I drove west over two very long days. I spent the night somewhere outside Twin Falls, Idaho. I'd planned to spend more time in Idaho, but it was the wrong season. Snow was coming, and I didn't want to get stranded.

I went to a bar that night after unpacking. I knew I had to get on the road early because of the snowstorm, and I wanted to see just a little bit of the town. For once, it was a quaint little place. I was feeling bored and a little lonely, one of the first times I had felt this way on my trip. It might be fun, just to visit with locals.

The bar was dark and dingy. The tables and chairs were scuffed, and there was an old jukebox in the corner. Lots of locals. I decided to risk taking off my mask. I felt safe.

As I walked toward the bar, my shoes stuck to the floor. Despite the dinginess and stickiness, there was a comfortable and cozy atmosphere. Not exactly a dive bar, but more like a local pub. No pretentiousness, just familiarity.

I sat at the bar and ordered a dirty, dry vodka martini with extra olives. At least six. I loved eating the olives between sips. One olive per sip was my goal. I grimaced as the alcohol hit my tongue. *Whoa.* It was strong. A few sips later, I was thoroughly relaxed.

I glanced around the bar. There were some tables scattered throughout the single room. A few couples, a table of young men, and two women intimately talking. *Prob-*

ably about men. I always presumed women were talking about men when they looked that serious. *That's what we do.* The bar area itself was empty. I saw the table of men glance toward the two women and laugh. The women were oblivious to the flirting. They must have been discussing something deeply important about men.

"Hello," said a voice to my left.

I jumped, startled.

I turned to see a man holding a single red rose.

"For you, a woman of magnificent beauty," he said.

I blushed, surprised at my reaction. I don't usually blush so easily. Or at least I didn't like to blush so easily.

I politely told him I wasn't interested.

"Oh," he said. "I'm just here to give you a rose. I don't want anything in return."

Now that was even more surprising. *Or he's a liar.*

I asked him if he made a habit out of giving strange women roses without any ulterior motives.

He laughed.

"How do you know? My secret plan may be that I am pretending to not have a motive.," he replied cryptically.

Now I was intrigued. The mystery. There it was, right in front of me. I couldn't walk away from the opportunity to delve deeply into a new, mysterious man.

"I have a story about a rose," I told him.

He smiled.

"There are many stories about roses," he said, "and most have happy endings."

I doubted that. The thorns will always get you.

I decided to play along.

I smiled and asked him. "What is a happy ending for you?"

"This isn't about me. This is about you. And your happy ending," he replied.

I don't have a happy ending. I wanted to say it out loud but decided it best to keep it to myself. Why expose all my deep, dark emotions? I decided it would be more fun to just continue to enjoy the game.

"I see," I replied. "Well, I don't need a happy ending. I already have one."

He laughed, handing me the rose, and ordered a beer.

"Another drink?" he asked.

I hesitated.

"Sure," I replied.

What the hell. I had nothing to do anyway, and I was enjoying his mischievous sense of humor. *Mischievousness.* I should add that to my non-negotiable list.

I tried to read him, to figure him out. Was he flirting or just an interesting person? Or maybe a dangerous person? I sensed I was safe.

He continued looking straight ahead, smiling.

"What do you see in my soul?" he asked me.

He knew I was reading him.

I didn't like being caught. I knew it was an intrusion into someone's personal space.

I smiled back at him and held my hands up in a gesture of surrender. I liked that he knew I was trying to read him, which surprised me because I always wanted to have the upper hand. Normally, I would have been bothered if someone knew I was trying to read them. But of course, he wasn't a date, and I had only just met him. If we were on a date, things would've been different.

I wanted to tell him I only sensed fearlessness. That's it. Or maybe it was confidence. Whatever it was, he didn't appear to have any fears. I was usually good at finding those. I decided it was likely he knew what I was thinking anyway. He was probably just as intuitive. No point spelling anything out.

I wondered, *Maybe he is the perfect man?* Someone, at least, who could apply for the position? I hated that I turned everything into romance, even a strange man offering me a rose in a dingy bar in a small town in Idaho.

My drink arrived and I took a sizeable sip. Clear and crisp. I had to slow down. This one was just as strong.

"I can't figure you out. You seem calm and fearless. But everyone has fears," I told him.

He slowly sipped his beer and said, "Maybe you're not as good at reading people as you think."

I knew I was good at reading people. And I knew that he knew that. Why was he playing games?

Maybe this was a bad idea.

"Look," I said, as I handed him back his rose, "I'm truly flattered, but I'm not interested."

"As I already said, I'm not here to flirt. Keep it. It belongs to you. Tell me your rose story," he said, looking at me with genuine interest.

I told him the story of the rose with the thorns and the metaphor for love and taking risks. After I finished, I turned to him and said, "But I'm not sure the rose is worth the risk. Too much pain."

"Have you given up, then?" he asked.

I wasn't even sure I knew the answer to that. *Had* I given up? I was dying, so there was nothing to give up by choice. It would've been amazing to have a love for my last few months, but I realized that was probably a mistake. My quest for the perfect man was really not about the man anyway. Given up?

No. *Maybe in my next life,* I wanted to say. But I wasn't sure he would understand. Where is love, anyway?

"Love is all around us," he said, reading my mind.

"Love isn't just about romance. It's about friendship and family and the love of the self."

The song "Love is All Around" popped into my head. I remembered the cheesy version from the movie *Love Actually.* Catchy song. Although I loved the movie, I detested it at the same time. I wanted that happy ending, and it seemed impossible and unrealistic. The stuff of fantasy. Concoctions of society. I was angry because I had given up hope of being happy in love. Why should everyone else be so happy? I recognized the movie was not reality. Many things we see, read, and hear about what love should be like are warped. And we know that. Yet we fall into the trap of desiring that fiction. Sometimes I wish I was more naïve, like a child, believing in dreams of love. I realized I could be if I wanted to. Maybe I could find a balance between fantasy and reality. I didn't think I could survive without hope. But I felt hope had been my downfall. Everything was so entangled. I wasn't sure I could tell the difference between false hope and real hope. Is hope neither false nor real? Is it just plain hope?

"What are you thinking about?" he asked.

"Hope," I replied.

"Remember, there's a difference between hope and expectations. There is no such thing as false hope," he answered.

I knew all that, but it still seemed like hope and expectations were the same things at times.

"Keep the rose," he said as he stood up and turned toward the door.

At that moment, the rose shined brightly. I picked it up off the counter and the flower expanded into a heart shape. Hearts and love. Love of everything and love of self. I felt an instant peace in my own heart, as if the blooming rose had caused my own heart to expand.

Love is all around.

I needed to ask the man about the rose and who he was. I ran to the door, hoping to catch up with him, but as I looked out into the dark street, he was gone. Whoever he was, he'd brought a powerful message, one that I already knew but seemed to forget in difficult times. Hope and love. Love and hope. Perhaps there was more to life than just men.

No, not perhaps. It was true. I already knew that. I just had to keep reminding my heart.

Everything would be okay.

HOPE

Journal Entry

There is a fine line between hope and expectation. I'm not sure I believe in false hope. I did, though, for a long time. Hope is hope, and it's necessary. It's never false. If we lose hope, how do we continue living? Hoping for love is real and positive. Expecting love is completely different. I know when manifesting, you're supposed to believe you already have the thing you want. That doesn't work for love. I'm not even convinced it works for anything. I think the Universe only brings you things that are for your highest good, even if they are bad. You learn through the challenges. Maybe it was in someone's highest good to get a million dollars. Maybe they had to learn a lesson. Like all those people who win the lottery and spend the money in a short time and end up penniless. The Law of Attraction is different—it's more about exuding positivity and love, and in the process, drawing more positivity into your life. If you're negative and always complaining, you'll just get more of the same.

Expecting someone to love you is pointless. People have free will and are complicated. But can you hope someone loves you? Yes, I think you can. But I have to be willing to hope, and then let it all go. Release the expectations. Live life and not dwell on it. If it doesn't happen, it's not the end of the world.

I expected him to love me. I didn't just hope for it. I expected it. And then I was disappointed when it didn't happen. I expected a relationship, a companion, someone to share my life. Because I'd felt something. I'd felt a connection, and I'd wanted it to work out so desperately. The desperation had created huge expectations for something that could never happen. He was broken. I was broken. Whether it was meant to be or not is irrelevant if two people are too broken to come together.

I've learned that hope is necessary, but I can't let it consume me. The death of my relationship felt like the death of hope, and that's why it was so hard to let go. But it was the end of expectations, what I had imagined would happen, the happily ever after I'd created in my head. I want to hope for a beautiful future and deeply connected love. I will release expectations.

What do I hope for now? I hope for love. All around.

COASTING TOWARD
THE PACIFIC

I left Idaho and the small town early the next morning. The rose was on my dashboard, still somehow looking fresh, without a single wilted petal. I planned to press it into a special book once I arrived home. *The Alchemist*? I would decide later. For now, I was simply enjoying its beauty and was basking in the hope that it promised. Hope for what, I didn't know, but just absorbing the hope was enough.

The mountain roads made for a longer trip, and I was very slow and cautious going downhill because of the grinding noises every time I braked too fast. I coasted a lot whenever I could. The noises were constant now, and I was worried.

Everything will be okay.

I pulled into my Airbnb on the outskirts of Seattle late at night and unpacked. I immediately fell asleep. Exhaustion and fearlessness. I was no longer afraid to be alone.

I woke up at three-thirty a.m., momentarily confused about where I was. I opened my eyes and for a second thought I was still with the bear man.

Where am I? My bed was empty except for my little corner near the edge. I must have slept without moving at all. In the dark, everything looked unfamiliar. It wasn't the bear man's cabin. I turned on the nightstand light, and then

I remembered. I was relieved not to wake up with another man. Bear man was enough for this trip. However beautiful, I didn't want to repeat any past patterns.

I couldn't get back to sleep. My mind was spinning as I thought through the experiences of the past few days. That I could love someone else. That I could trust someone again. I'd trusted bear man. He'd saved my life and kept me warm. Only for a short time, but the warmth stayed with me. I tried to force myself to sleep but decided I should probably just get up and have some coffee. Maybe I would write.

CONFUSION IN WRITING

Journal Entry

I have a multitude of ideas in my head. Too many things to write about. Too many stories. I need to focus. One is almost done, but something is missing. It sounds childish.

Nothing feels right in any of my drafts. Just stories empty of emotion. Safe. Things to help me escape my fears. I had a strange thought the other day, that everything I write comes true. Maybe I need to write happy endings. My last book didn't have a happily-ever-after-woman-gets-man ending, but it sent an empowering message of strength and independence. Still, it was a beautiful ending. A fairytale ending doesn't seem real, and yet I'm writing with that intention in mind. I created this character as an extension of myself, planning to give her the ending she deserves. I want that ending, too. But I don't have it and I can't. Maybe if I write a happy ending it will come true for me. More craziness. Can I change my life? Can I prevent death?

The most important thing I should be looking at is the mountain man. I sat in the car for hours driving west, wondering if he was real. Then I would touch the pendant around my neck and confirm he was. A mysterious experience. But there's no happy ending. He's gone just as surely as all the others.

I can't want anything. As soon as I desire something, it goes away. Except for my desire to free myself from his memory. I desire that release, yet it stays. Maybe I'm not supposed to be happy. Everything is the opposite of how I want things to be. I don't think I'm any closer to releasing everything and being healed than I was when I left the east coast. Just more memories to add to the already overly-stuffed storage space in my head.

I fear.

I'm cold.

I'm lonely. Always. Even with a man. Except for the mountain man. Maybe.

And yet, the experience freed me from some of my fears. I still feel his warmth. My thoughts are the opposite of what I write. Usually, things flow. Is this my heart talking? Which is the truth? My mind or my heart? What comes through when I write?

Nothing makes sense to me. Writing always makes me feel better, yet right now, it made me feel worse.

Uncomfortable truths.

I want comfort, warmth, and protection.

WILD MAN
FROM THE SEA

I felt a little despondent after writing. Not at all what usually happens. Writing usually helps me release my feelings and ultimately makes me feel better. I knew there was more I needed to release, to write about, but I was avoiding it. *I know what I fear and why I'm cold-hearted and lonely.* Later. I would think about it later. In truth, I did feel better after my encounter with the mountain man. I felt as if I'd released something, even if my journal wasn't in agreement. I always believed what I wrote came from my heart, but maybe sometimes the words came from my mind, the constant desire for logical answers, that then evolved into persistent arguments with my heart. More to think about. *I just need to feel.*

The sun finally came up, and I headed to the coast just south of my cottage. I wanted to explore. I would be joyful at the ocean. I loved the sea and the peace it instilled.

I didn't have a location in mind. I just drove until I found a place to park near the ocean. I hiked down a sandy path to the water. It was a cold fall day, and the ocean was wild and wonderful. The waves crashed against the rocky shore, and the thunderous sound blocked out all negative thoughts. I sat on a rock, closed my eyes, and just listened, stopping the chatter in my head and the entanglement in my heart. I felt the vibration of each wave. The sea spoke to me, telling me all was well. I was at peace.

My peace was broken by a shout. I opened my eyes and looked around, but saw nothing. Again, I heard the voice. A male voice, but I couldn't make out the words. Whoever he was, he was far away. I looked out to the sea and scanned the horizon, and in the distance, I saw a sailboat. It was far away—I wasn't sure the voice was even coming from there. I couldn't see anything clearly without my glasses. The boat sailed closer, and I thought I saw a man waving. As the boat came into clearer focus, I thought I saw his mouth move and the word *hey* escape from his lips. I stood up and sent him a friendly wave in return.

The boat continued toward shore, then turned north along the shoreline. I walked over the rocks, following the boat, wondering where he was going.

I loved the idea of sailing. When I was younger, I'd dreamt of sailing around the world in a tiny sailboat. That dream ended when I realized I feared drowning. Strange to desire things and yet be scared at the same time. That explained many things about my life.

I followed the boat, hoping for a sailing adventure. *No fear.* This time, I would go and sail to wherever the boat was going!

As I turned the corner, the sailboat was navigating into a small cove. I continued along the sandy path, picking up my pace because he was almost there. I was curious to hear where he had come from and where he was going. A fellow adventurer, one much braver than myself. *I am brave. I will sail with him!*

He dropped anchor and I watched him get into his dinghy. He rowed quickly toward shore. As he approached,

I noticed his hair. His beard. He looked like he had been shipwrecked. Or he was homeless. Wild hair everywhere, unshaven and darkly tanned, with a weathered face. I did a double-take. There was something about him that seemed familiar, but I couldn't figure out where I knew him from. Maybe it was a dream. *Why does everyone seem so familiar?*

I stood still, waiting for him. He lugged the boat onto the sand and turned, looking right at me—not a glance, but a deep stare. I looked at him but quickly turned away. I felt his stare and that he could see me, *really see me*. I kept myself well-protected. I didn't like the intrusion. But I hoped that was in the past. His look felt slightly uncomfortable but also incredibly exciting. *Not many men see me.* As he got closer, I could see his eyes were brown and dark. Were they sad? Or were they understanding? I couldn't figure him out. Just very intense and full of knowledge, as well as deep emotion. The eyes are everything to me. You can read so much about a person by gazing into their eyes.

He knew me. I thought it was funny that this man, who looked so disheveled, had captured my attention. All because of the eyes. And the fact that he knew me. I felt he did. I was intrigued. I smiled and nodded my head in a greeting of sorts. Being polite, being something…

He suddenly started running toward me. I was wary and a little nervous.

"Good morning," he bellowed, a serious look on his face.

"Hello," I replied. Polite and distant. *Maybe I shouldn't get too close, be too friendly.*

"Oh, I forgot," he quickly turned around and returned to the dinghy, grabbing an old sack.

He walked up to me and said he had something that belonged to me. He untied the dirty, old-looking sack, pulled out a deep blue bottle, and handed it to me. I was confused. I wasn't sure what he wanted me to do with the bottle. I held it up and noticed there was something inside.

"This is for me?" I asked, wondering why he thought this was mine.

"Open it," he said.

I was excited. I'd always wanted a message in a bottle. I wanted to open it and find out what the message said. I stopped questioning why he said it was for me.

I tried to pull off the cork, but I wasn't strong enough. It was stuck. I tried a different angle, and still no luck. He smiled and took the bottle from me, easily pulling the cork out with his strong, calloused hands. Was he another rugged mountain man? No, he was a seaman. A wild sailor, a wanderer of the seven seas. He handed me back the bottle and I flipped it upside down, a small scrap of paper falling into my palm.

I unrolled it and read the words.

I've been searching my entire life for you. You, the woman who does not have faith. I'm coming soon. Will you please wait?

Then the wild man knelt in front of me, opening his arms wide in a gesture of surrender. I was confused. Was this note from him?

"Wait. Did you write this?" I asked.

He shrugged. *How could he not know?* If it wasn't him, then who was this message from? Was he a messenger? Was he a spirit? I wanted to understand, but I needed to know more.

"Where is this message from?" I asked, hoping that he could, or would, answer the question.

He pointed up. I looked up, not sure what I expected to see. Another message from an airplane? I saw nothing but the sun rising into a blue sky.

"Why did you give me this message?" I wanted answers and at that point probably sounded irate.

I didn't mean to sound upset, but I was confused and didn't understand what it all meant. I hated not knowing things.

He took my hand and gestured toward the boat. Anyone in their right mind would have walked away. But I wasn't in my right mind and let him lead me to the dinghy and back to his boat. What's the worst that could happen? *A lot.* I knew in my heart I would be okay.

Once on board, he started talking. He told me some stories. Long detailed and fascinating stories of his adventures. He had sailed around the world several times over the past twenty years. The boat was his home.

The more he talked, though, the more disjointed his stories became. They soon made little sense. He spoke of the death of his mother and father in a terrible accident when he was twelve and how he had been on his own since then. At first, he'd walked around the world but then found sailing was easier and safer. He said he'd met many presidents. At each place he stopped, they all wanted to meet the man who'd walked around the world. It all seemed like a fantasy, a dream. *Maybe he's insane.*

I wanted to hear about the bottle.

"Tell me about the bottle," I pleaded.

He said he'd found the bottle when he was crossing the Atlantic. A storm had just come through and it was bobbing next to his boat. He had plucked it out of the water and opened it, finding the mysterious note inside. He knew it wasn't meant for him. He knew the note was meant for someone, but he didn't know who, so he put the note back in the bottle and kept sailing, searching for the recipient of the message.

A crazy story. But I believed every word.

"How do you know it's meant for me?" I asked.

"Because God told me," he replied assuredly.

Oh no. He was crazy. I believed in many things, so why didn't I believe that God had told him this note was meant for me? My words *I believe in everything* echoed back to me. I needed to believe him, or that would mean I had no faith. It all sounded crazy, but maybe it made perfect sense. I just didn't understand yet.

I read the note again. Over and over, hoping to gain some insight or at least get an intuitive ping about its meaning. So many questions. Who has been searching for me? And why? How does he (I presumed it was a *he*) know I don't have faith? He was coming and he was asking me to wait.

"Can God tell you anything else?" I asked.

"I don't know for sure. Can I see the message?" he asked.

I was surprised.

"You haven't read it?" I asked.

"It wasn't my message." He shrugged. "I looked at it but didn't unroll it. I put it back in the bottle."

I handed him the note and asked, "Can you ask God the meaning of this message? Does God know who this person is who is searching for me?"

He unrolled the paper and read the message.

"God's not speaking to me right now. He only speaks when He feels like it." He handed the paper back to me. "Maybe later."

Great. I'd have to wait to get any answers. Most likely, it would be never. He was just a madman sailing around the world carrying an old glass bottle with a secret message for anyone.

"Later? What do you mean? I need answers now!" I was pleading at this point. The words came out full of intense emotion.

"I'm sorry," he said as he walked over and handed me the bottle. "It's yours."

Our eyes locked. There was a deep intensity, as if he had something of great significance to share. Then he said it. He said my name. I hadn't shared my name with him at any point. There was no way he could know my name. He smiled. I didn't.

Then he said something that would change my entire perspective.

He spoke truth and love and pain and wisdom. Then he said I wasn't allowed to share his words with anyone. Not yet.

I was overwhelmed.

"How do you know all of this?" I asked in a whisper.

He pointed towards the sky. *God.*

I cried gigantic baby tears. I had dragged so many sorrows behind me for too long. They followed me everywhere, and I was tired. I wanted to set them down.

He came near me and hugged me, pulling me close.

I was so caught up in the moment, I suddenly wanted him. I turned my face toward him and kissed him. He didn't kiss me back and gently pushed me away.

"No. This is not the meaning of this," he said gently.

I was hurt. I wanted him, but he didn't want me. I know he saw the disappointment on my face.

"Don't you understand? After what I just told you, you can't be with any man. For now."

I understood. But I still wanted him. I was weak, but I nodded my head and told him I understood. No more men. For now. Not forever. Just for now. *How long*? I needed to find the perfect man before I died.

"It's time to go," he said, handing me my bottle with the note safely tucked inside.

He rowed me back to shore. I stared at the bottle the entire time, still wondering how the note was connected to the message the wild man had told me. It was yet another riddle to be added to my collection.

He hugged me goodbye and told me, "It's time to go. Go back, go home."

Home? I didn't have a home. *Home is where the heart is.* My heart is everywhere and nowhere.

I stood watching him row back to his boat. I watched as he prepared his sails and set out back into the ocean, back to wherever it was he'd come from. I watched until he was a speck on the horizon, growing smaller and smaller until I could no longer see him with my weak eyes.

BACK TO THE PAST

Despite feeling not ready to return east, I did. It took me four days. As I drew closer, I grew more anxious and unhappy. I was supposed to have healed, but I felt worse. This trip was supposed to have helped me find what I was looking for. Was it a bottle? A secret message? I had no idea. I only felt sadness as the days passed. My adventure was almost over, and I didn't know what I would do next.

I felt as if I was backtracking, not moving forward. I thought to myself, *I'm headed back to a place I don't belong.* I was returning a failure. I'd failed in my quest. I'd expected to be a nomad for a while, wandering and exploring. I wanted to be somewhere I hadn't been. If I didn't have the answers, that's where they would be. The old places had no answers for me.

By the time I arrived home, the words of the wild man were less clear. I'd thought I understood what he meant. But now, being back in the same place, I was stuck. His message seemed meaningless. I was waiting for something to happen, something that would change my life.

Death?

I was annoyed with myself. Annoyed at being back, annoyed at everyone around me. I wanted to move forward so badly, to who knows what, but I was stuck, firmly glued to my temporary, sedentary existence. Time moved slowly, and I was afraid I was in this frozen cycle forever. I became a hermit, not wanting to see people, not wanting to do much of anything. It was winter and cold, and I wasn't sure where I was going on my life path. Was I a healer? A writer? Things that had once worked out so easily for me—writing projects and other side gigs—seemed to be falling apart, while other potential opportunities slipped away, no matter how hard I tried.

I grew worried, which was foreign to me, because I always knew *everything was going to be okay*. I kept telling myself that, and I knew it in my heart, but the worry overcame me. Bad things were happening to people I loved, and somehow, I blamed myself. My negative thinking was the cause of everything. I needed to be more positive. So hard to do when you feel like everything around you is falling apart. I knew I just needed to flow, but I wasn't even sure what that meant anymore.

I was lonely. I desperately wanted to go out on a date. With anyone. I didn't even care what they did or what they looked like. I needed to find a way to fill the emptiness that appeared to be overtaking me. Dating seemed like a good option. Then I remembered the words of the wild man from the sea. No dating. For now. I was still communicating with Alan, the man I'd been seeing before I left. He seemed so ordinary compared to the men I had met on my adventures. I still wanted a mountain man. I wanted my bear mountain man. It all seemed too long ago.

But what did *for now* mean? It could've meant while I was traveling. I tried to convince myself that's what it meant. However, I realized intuitively that it meant for a longer period.

How will I know when it's time?

THE ENDS OF THE EARTH

I pondered my woeful existence and sat in self-pity longer than I wanted to. *I could not accept the pity of others yet found it so easy to pity myself.* A conundrum. Another realization.

Just in time, I was saved by a friend. She called and told me someone she knew was taking a small group to Peru the following week and they had a last-minute cancellation. She asked if I wanted to take the open spot. I didn't hesitate. I'd always wanted to go, but the timing was never right. Plus, I wasn't sure I wanted to travel alone. This was the perfect opportunity, and I immediately said yes. I bought a very expensive plane ticket and packed my bags. I filled my Xanax prescription. The irony—the woman who loves to travel has a horrendous fear of flying. There you go. Alanis: *that* is irony. I had tried everything, and it was the only thing that worked for me. One pill and I had no cares in the world. If I could have taken one every day perhaps, I would have been a more balanced person. *No. I didn't need it.* I had so much growth through my pain and turmoil. I was energized and finally looked toward the future with hope. Not hope for love but hope to clear the remnants of whatever was drowning me.

I still didn't quite understand what was holding me back and how I was still stuck, at times, thinking about him and the possibilities. I was getting some strange intuitive nudges, which I discounted. I realized I no longer fully trusted my intuition. I understood my mistakes in the past and how I'd ignored my intuition. However, my intuition was needling me with things about him, things I didn't want to know about. Nothing definite, just words that I didn't want to believe or follow. *Patience. Wait. Healing.* I wasn't sure what these words meant. I had been patiently waiting to heal. I was working on myself and had come a long way. I was trying to release the past. But then why was his name popping up during those times? Perhaps to remind me of what I was trying to release. For one split second, I thought the words were telling me to wait for him. I knew that was wrong. I disregarded it as remnants of the pain. I needed to be patient with my healing. It would take time. *Patience* was my new mantra.

I hoped this would be a life-changing trip. I knew it would be, so I wasn't worried about having false expectations. A knowing. This intuitive ping I accepted. The ones about him, I would never again accept. There would be no more waiting or believing we would be together. I didn't care what the Universe was telling me. When it came to him, I was wrong. My intuition was wrong. So I brushed it away. Never again would I trust anything regarding him. It wasn't that I didn't trust the Universe. I just didn't trust myself.

The natural beauty and the spiritual experiences were powerful throughout the trip. I remember our first stop vividly. We visited an alpaca and llama farm where we had the opportunity to touch these beautiful creatures. People say that llamas are aggressive, but that wasn't true at all in this case. They just stood there as our group of strangers approached. As soon as I touched the soft, wooly coat of one of the smaller llamas, I felt instantly connected to nature—I felt the vibration of the animal and the energy that exists in the natural world. I moved to the next nearest animal and did the same thing. Again, the energy flowed through my fingers and through my physical and spiritual body, grounding itself back into the earth beneath my feet. An infinite circle of pure energy. The sense of peace and connectedness made me want to stay longer. While the others continued to explore the farm, I stayed with the llamas. In solitude, I felt more connected to the Universe than I had in a very long time.

I flowed. By the time we arrived at our first ancient mystical site, my vibration was higher and more positive. That was where we met the shaman, Don Diego, who would guide us on the rest of our trip. He changed my life. It sounded trite to even let those words pass through my mind. But it was true. Every experience, with him in the lead, brought me closer to balance and infused me with love—not only for myself, but for everyone and everything in existence. Peace and tranquility. I was exploding with love. Love for life, love for myself, love for the experience, and most of all, love for others as humans, not just as romantic possibilities, but as energetic connections that saturated me with a powerful sense of hope.

These powerful energetic experiences continued, but a key component of the trip was the amazing group of like-minded adventurers on the journey. My tribe. Everyone understood when I told them about my experience with the animals and the profound meditations at the mystical sites. They believed in synchronicities and the power that exists within us all. And more importantly, the deep connections to everything and to each other. We understood that there was a far deeper meaning to life than just living in the physical world. I finally felt I wasn't alone on my journey through life—I had connected to like-minded people who understood me and my beliefs. Our energetic, pure, loving connection permeated the entire experience. I was rainbows and unicorns the entire time, and it felt pure. I wanted to live like that all the time, even if I appeared naïve and childish. Having more of this in my life without having expectations seemed like a perfect balance. As I moved through the experience, I realized that negative thinking was my worst enemy. More likely, too much thinking in general had resulted in pain and kept me stuck. I shut off the inner dialogue, the endless chatter when I entered into meditation with nature. I wanted to hold on to these feelings for as long as possible. I told myself, *I will.* I was free.

Of course, there were some challenges on the trip. The altitude in certain places got to me. I was exhausted and out of breath with a constant, dull headache. It was worse than the Colorado mountains. I called room service and ordered oxygen so I could function. Such a humorous concept to me—to order up oxygen to my room. *Could you please bring me a sandwich and a canister of oxygen?* It worked though. I wished I had ordered it earlier in the trip. While most hotels in Cusco pumped oxygen into the rooms, it obviously wasn't enough.

The first night in Cusco, I woke up at three a.m. and went looking for some more coca tea, which helped with altitude sickness. The hotel had served us tea when we arrived in the afternoon, and I felt I needed more. I wandered down to the lobby, but unfortunately, they only had mint tea. Coca tea was only for daytime use, the woman in the lobby said. Too much caffeine. Coca, that's where cocaine comes from. Of course. I learned something new. I basically drank and ate cocaine leaves the entire trip. I knew it wasn't the same thing, but it made me feel rebellious. The reality was, the coca had little effect in its natural state.

I needed something. I felt terrible. So I reluctantly filled my cup with mint tea and headed back to my room for a sleepless night. I hoped I would grow accustomed to the altitude and return to normal, but I felt a little off the entire trip. It didn't matter though. Despite feeling ill, the moments of spiritual connectedness and growth were profound. Perhaps *because* I didn't feel great, the uncomfortableness forced me into a deeper state.

I wasn't disappointed with anything. I had no specific expectations. I had no time to conjure visions of myself bathed in the beauty of spiritual experiences in Peru. Every day, before and during the trip, I lived in the moment. Life was full of wondrous surprises when I had few expectations and released my worries about the future. And more importantly, let go of past regrets. I didn't understand how I arrived at the point of just being. It just happened.

Machu Picchu is a dream, I was told by the shaman. I could hardly believe I was there. It felt like a dream. Despite my altitude sickness, I was giddy. The wandering alpacas at the site—or were they llamas? Admittedly, I couldn't tell the difference. I loved them equally. Every single ancient site was a transcendental spiritual experience. Led by our shaman guide, we traveled from Machu Picchu to Lake Titicaca and many places in between.

As we sailed back to Puno from an island in the middle of Lake Titicaca, I had a final conversation with the shaman. Tomorrow we would fly back to Lima, and he would go on to his home. I asked him, *How do I find my true purpose in life?* I had many things I was interested in doing, and many of them spoke to my soul, but I wasn't sure if there should be only one or if I could somehow combine them. I felt scattered sometimes, with too many choices and the uncertainty of which was my true calling. I wanted a calling, something I would be passionate about. It would help me get past my desire for a man. I asked for his guidance.

He told me that he sensed love. That my learning and my teaching were about the heart and love. He said my heart was full of love and I needed to share that love.

"Open your heart," he said.

I did think about love a lot, but mostly it seemed to be about the failures. I gave love freely, openly, and without hesitation, but that was in the past, before going through all the pain and attempts to heal. I had closed myself off. I realized what he said resonated with me. I loved giving, sharing love, and making everyone feel the love. The past pain had forced me to decide my heart was too fragile for the world, and I'd tucked it away. Protecting myself. I didn't want to share it with anyone. I saw now that I did want to share it. I was just afraid.

He then handed me a greenish stone in the shape of a heart. He said the stone, serpentine, came from the mountains surrounding Machu Picchu, and he had harvested, carved, and polished it himself. He told me to keep it with me. It would bring me peace. The stone was shiny and felt cool to the touch. I grasped it tightly in my hand, held it up to my forehead, and took a deep inhale. I carefully tucked the stone in my pocket and smiled at him. Peace. I carried the stone heart with me the rest of the trip—in my backpack during the day and under my pillow at night.

I shifted my perspective. I was no longer an unfocused, lonely woman. I was confident, an empowered soul whose heart was slowly opening. I was also no longer just a solo soul. I was a woman with deep connections to other beautiful souls who understood the meaning of spirituality. I struggled but climbed a mountain. I overcame altitude sickness. I felt free and authentic. And I understood that I wasn't powerless.

I carried that feeling with me for many weeks, keeping the stone always in my possession, meditating daily, and staying in tune with nature.

TAKING FLIGHT

I had a dream on day ten of my return from Peru. I still felt balanced, but I had such a strong desire to return there. I hoped I could keep my balance.

In the dream, the shaman from Peru was standing before us, the same group from the trip. He said he had given each of us a gift at Lake Titicaca during the *despacho* ceremony. We had to discover what those gifts were on our own—he wasn't going to tell us. We couldn't tell anyone about our gifts. Not now. I wanted to know what my gift was.

Great. Another 'not now'! Was the Universe trying to teach me patience?

I stood there and looked up at the sky and suddenly found myself lifting off the ground. I was flying. I knew that was my gift. I flew high above the shaman and the group, feeling free and light, with no heaviness from my troubles. It was that wonderful feeling you get from flying dreams. I wanted to go farther, to see more, but the shaman urged me to come down.

"Nobody can know," he told me. *"It's not time."* I didn't want to come down. But I listened to him.

I couldn't completely understand the meaning of the dream. I even tried to make my waking self fly that morning. I closed my eyes and imagined myself going up, up, up. It didn't work. I mentioned my dream to a friend. If I was supposed to fly, why couldn't I? I believed I could.

Too much faith! She said maybe it was a metaphor. That's when it hit me. *Of course!* When I was flying, I was looking down on everyone and everything. I was seeing everything from a higher perspective. That was the message. To look at everything that had happened, was happening, and would happen from a higher, different perspective. Now that I understood, I needed to find out why. Was it from a universal perspective? A view of why things happened, not being so centered on self? Did everything that happened to me have more significant meaning than just to myself? It was a lot to think about. And I knew I wouldn't find the answers right away.

GRADUAL DECLINE

For a bit of time, I continued to feel the positivity from my trip. Then things seemed to fall apart. The house I was supposed to rent fell through. I couldn't find a permanent place to live, and I was longing to be on my own, not relying on anyone, having my own space. I was grateful my friend had opened her home to me, but I couldn't stay there anymore. Quite the opposite from when I'd started my nomadic adventure. I wanted a home again, a place to put my things that had been in storage for almost a year. It was time, but I was stuck. I felt trapped. There was nothing on the market, and I had nowhere to go and nothing to do since my writing had come to a screeching halt after I'd returned from my cross-country adventure. I needed a place to just be on my own for a few months, somewhere peaceful, where I could drift into death. Or maybe I should just go sit on Machu Picchu…rent a house nearby. But I didn't really want any of those things. I felt helpless and alone and in desperate need of saving. I needed to be saved! But who could save me?

HARD LESSONS

It was my fault. I let the worry, boredom, and insecurity drag me back down into the dating abyss.

I still wasn't free. I still thought about him and felt that longing that wouldn't go away. Despite my balance, and my new tribe, I crumbled. I didn't know what else to do to forget it but go back to my old habits. Dating was the only way I could forget. My quest for the perfect man made me forget. I hoped that somehow I would meet that man. Why was it so important, even though I was dying? Most people wouldn't care. I felt like I was pulled to do certain things, but they didn't make any sense. I was still trying to figure out the mystery of the blue bottle and the message from the wild man. I had no idea what any of it meant. And I was tired and scared.

I didn't go back to dating apps. I simply reached out to Alan. He hadn't texted me in quite a while. Was it too late? I decided to say hello. And we went on a date. There was a mild connection, but I was still unsure. I wasn't afraid. It was more of an intuitive ping that I chose to ignore yet again. I had spoken to a friend about him, and she told me to just go for it. I wasn't getting any younger. *Some friend, right?*

We had fun, going on travel adventures and eating out. Spending a lot of time together. But I didn't have any feelings for him. Nothing at all. I felt like a cold, heartless person because I could tell he had feelings for me. I would decide one day that I was breaking up with him, but then I would go out with him the next without enthusiasm. He was very convincing. He was exuberant and promised a great time. I kept wondering what the purpose was of continuing to see him. And why, if he wasn't right for me, the Universe hadn't said anything or sent a sign. Was my uncertainty enough? Did I need the guidance of the Universe when I already knew in my heart that he wasn't the man for me?

During all of this, two men I had dated a long time ago reached out to me. Men I had feelings for—if not love, at least a deep attraction. I was tempted, but then the ping in my intuition told me to avoid them. I listened this time. Still, something felt off with Alan. I felt as if I was just going through the motions of dating. He was great. Kind, thoughtful, stable, secure, financially secure…my life was crumbling around me, I had no independence and was living off my savings. I decided he was a good enough catch. *Good enough* was a terrible thing to admit. I didn't love him, nor even like him that much. He was just a friend. I had asked to be saved. Maybe that's why he came. But I didn't want to be saved by him, and I knew I had to save myself. I wasn't sure what to do. Then I had a dream.

He was there. My lost love, standing right next to me holding my hand. He looked right into my eyes and said, "*I'm coming.*"

In my dream, I wasn't surprised. I told him, "*I know.*"

"*Then why are you wasting your time with someone you don't love,*" he asked.

"*Because I'm scared of dying alone.*"

He hugged me and said, "*You're not alone. Just wait a little longer, please. Stop dating. It's messing everything up.*"

I woke up believing it was true. After all my screwed-up intuitive decisions and inner turmoil, I believed he was coming. Then I stopped myself. Maybe it's not him. Maybe someone else is coming. I couldn't one hundred percent believe he was coming. That would have been too much faith. A miracle. I saw it as guidance, telling me to stop dating because it wasn't healthy for me. I would have something I wanted eventually, but I had to stop dating. It was messing me up spiritually and emotionally. Or it was messing something else up? I didn't like this dream. It just put me back on the path of confusion.

Over the next few weeks, the visions and dreams increased, and he was always there. Mostly he would just stand in the background, wave at me, or just sit and stare. Sometimes the voice of the Universe, like a voiceover, would boom, "*I can't help you if you're sad. I can't help you if keep getting involved with men.*" Yes, being involved with men made me sad. I understood the message.

Nevertheless, my mind wandered. I had dated to mask the pain and to find someone to replace him. What if everything I had done, including walking away from him, had been wrong? It was a mutual walking away, but I'd never been patient with anything, even though the Universe was trying to tell me to be patient. But he had walked away from me, that much was clear. I didn't understand what I was supposed to be patient about. As I read through my journals, I saw the many messages I'd received about patience. It wasn't just his fault, the screwed-up, messy relationship we'd had. It was also mine. *Or am just misinterpreting everything again? No,* came a voice. *You never misinterpreted anything. You just purposefully made the wrong choices. You lost faith.*

I lost faith. Yes, anyone would have. He left. He walked away. I kept trying, hoping, and praying to no avail. I was defensive when I saw him. I blamed him for everything when we'd both made mistakes, and I said things that I shouldn't have said. As I said these words to myself, they sounded crazy. *No, I couldn't believe any of this. I was never to blame.*

Despite the constant bombardment of messages, I refused to believe any of it was true. It wasn't a question of faith—it was about acceptance. It was over and done, and he had moved on. It had been years since we'd even spoken to each other, and I was doing my best to move forward. I had to stand in my truth. I loved him, but he didn't love me, and he'd walked away. I tried everything, too many things, to make things work, and perhaps the real answer was the Universe had deceived me at every turn. The Universe had told me we were meant to be. The Universe had told me to go toward him, to keep trying. And it had ended in horrible pain and a deep stuckness of false hope. I refused to walk that path again. I was angry at the Universe for continuing to tell me lies.

And I was angry at Alan, even though none of it was his fault. I was angry at all men for not loving me, and ultimately, I was angry at myself for falling so deeply and then spending so much time digging myself out of the abyss. I told the Universe, "*I'm done.*" Done with men, done with dating, done with faith, done with hope. *I'm tired. So very tired.* Tired of living. I wasn't suicidal, I didn't want to die, but I was tired. The weight of everything made me want to just crawl into a hole and hide. The only thing that saved me from continuing down a dark path was that I had little time to live. I kept thinking I'd be free soon enough.

AUTOPSY OF MY LOVE

Part of releasing the past means to stop fervently obsessing about something. Or someone. Stop thinking about it—him—repetitively. If in every moment of the present, you continue to be consumed with the memories of the past, you are lost. You look for distraction. I wanted answers. I felt I couldn't release him until I had put myself back together. Until I knew exactly what had gone wrong and whether I had done everything I could to put things back together. Why couldn't I put it all back together? I must have done something wrong. I rarely failed at anything. If I wanted something, I got it. That's just how my life had been.

From our first meeting, I looked back at every small, little detail. Where were the red flags? I already knew the answer to that. Yes. Huge, blood-red flags. Signs. Omens. Warnings. It was obvious the Universe was trying to warn me to stay away from him. It should have been clear, right? I would think it would have been clear to anyone. But that's the problem with hindsight. Back then, I wasn't looking for red flags, and events were just coincidences instead of signs or warnings. They were meaningless, trivial events.

Were there other things I didn't see besides the blatantly obvious? I wasn't in tune with myself back then, but I did sense in him a mysterious seriousness. It was only mysterious because I didn't understand it and the seriousness, I know now, was sadness. That's why I didn't want to see him again after that first meeting. He hardly smiled, and he kept looking at his drink or his hands, talking slowly and only occasionally looking up. I knew something wasn't right, but for me, it was a matter of personality, not spirit. He wasn't right for me. I wanted someone more lively, more fun. And I made the decision not to see him again. And yet, I did.

And the rest is, well, tragedy.

What if I had said no to the second date? I know, the terrible torturous "what if." Not only had I done it when I made decisions about the future, but sometimes I looked at the past and asked myself: What if I had done things differently? It's not that I was filled with regret. It became a story, a different story of a different person who had walked onto a different timeline. I loved imagining a different future for myself. Or that I was living that other future now in an alternate reality. The things I missed out on weren't lost if I could create a new story in my mind. What if I had been braver and sailed around the world when I had the chance? What if I hadn't married when I did? What if I had slept with that director when I was an actress in New York? I imagined a life vastly different than the one I was currently living. I pretended it was for fun, but I wasn't happy in my timeline, so I sought happiness elsewhere. I assembled it for myself, imagining a whole other existence.

As I examined the past, particularly my love for him and my insistence that he love me, I sought to find answers. I was lovable, after all. I was special. Of course, I had been rejected before. I had been hurt before. Like everyone in life, I too suffered pain. But this had been different, and I needed to know why I still carried it with me into every relationship. This examination required deep cuts. I wasn't sure I was ready. I preferred to just play the game of what if.

I knew I needed to do something. I was stuck in a loop. Picking the same type of emotionally unavailable men. Men I never wanted in my life before being ripped apart by his lack of love. But I not only chose men of that type, but I somehow also found that those men had the same color eyes as him or the same love for classical music, and some even had similar body shapes and mannerisms. Sometimes even the same type of career or childhood. I didn't know most of these things before I met them. And then when they surfaced, I understood them to be a sign of some sort. At that point, I was looking for signs every-where. Everything was a sign. Nothing was a coincidence. I was supposed to meet these men, supposed to have some connection with them. Why? I had no idea. Those connections between the men were signs. They became mysterious moments that I couldn't escape instead of what they were—the search for love.

The search for him.

THE CELIBATE HERMIT

A new place to live fell into my lap. I had given up hope, and then out of the blue, I found a small cottage in the country to rent. I moved in, setting up the house as much as possible. Too many things and so little space was frustrating. I needed to get rid of more stuff. But I was happy in my solitude.

I mostly stayed home. No dating, of course. I sometimes saw friends and family. I ran errands, exercised, and started writing again. I also broke up with Alan. Once I released him and stopped my incessant inner chatter with the Universe, it was a very peaceful time. I only interacted with people who were balanced, thoughtful, and nonjudgmental. Friends who wouldn't mock me when I told them I was taking some time, a break, to do some inner work. To be completely by myself without a man. No dating. That was a big thing for me. It had been very hard for me to not date. In a way, Covid gave me a great excuse to take myself out of dating. Nobody was dating back then. It was safe to say no.

During the pandemic, I focused on myself. I finished my first book in record time. It was taking me forever to finish the second one. I just couldn't write. I didn't feel it for a long time. I was so annoyed with myself. But at the same time, I kept telling myself that there must be a deeper meaning. The timing. It wasn't yet time to finish my book. That gave me peace. I would write whenever I felt like it. Whenever I was moved by a great idea or a clever title. Like the *Celibate Hermit*. Or the *Hermitic Celibate*. Of course, shouldn't hermits be celibate? Not necessarily. Maybe. I guess it depends on how you define celibacy. Is it just abstaining from sex or not interacting with men at all? As in, no official dating.

I still craved that feeling of *the date*. That excitement, the buildup. Yes, I know it usually ended in disappointment. It was a crapshoot. Like gambling. I loved being seen. I wanted to be seen and admired. I knew how to dress, how to smile, and what to say. I felt so confident. And superior. Like I was interviewing them for a job and there was no way they would meet the standards of my fifty-plus, non-negotiable requirements. *I should make them write cover letters.*

Locking myself up felt like a waste. Dating gave me joy. *If it doesn't give you joy, get rid of it.* But sometimes things that supposedly give you joy are a lie. It's a trick. The joy they give is merely comfort or safety, a crutch. I felt safe dating. Strange, wasn't it? I wondered why dating made me feel safe. I didn't understand that it made me feel safe and that I needed it. Even when it was annoying and boring and weird. I craved it. I was addicted.

Even the weird dates. One guy I met ran into his ex and asked if she would join us for a drink. I don't care how friendly you are with your ex. You don't have them sit with you and your new first date. He'd asked if I minded. I should have said no, but part of me was curious as to how this would play out. Maybe I would learn something about him. I learned he was boring and still very much attached to his ex. He sat closer to her than he did to me. I listened to them talk, being ignored. That was fun. When he asked me for a second date, I told him *no thanks*. I didn't bother to tell him why. He seemed so clueless. He probably wouldn't even have understood.

Or the man who wanted to have sex in his car on our first date. Maybe I'm a prude, but no way. Must have been a long time for him. He must have been desperate. Poor guy. Not for me, thanks. Speaking of sex, I went on a date with a guy who asked me about my toes. No lie. First date. He said he loved toes, and it was important for him to see my toes right away. It was winter and I had my boots on. I wasn't about to take off my boots and show him my toes in the restaurant. He asked me to come up to his apartment which was right around the corner. Again with the immediate sex. Really? He couldn't come up with a more creative or romantic gesture to get me into bed? Maybe he does get bonus points for creativity. I've never been asked to show my toes on a first date. I said *no thanks, not for me. My toes are my own and I don't want to share them with you.* I wonder what his non-negotiable list looked like. Creepy?

Then there was angry man. Every bit as angry as you could imagine. Angry at the world, angry at himself, and then turning his anger toward me. He seemed so kind and balanced when we'd chatted before our date. We had a lot in common, including that we were both angry at others for our own choices. At least I was able to see in him how I felt sometimes. Angry that things weren't working out for me in love, angry that I had been rejected. Angry that I always seemed to choose the wrong person. He opened my eyes. While I would never express myself as he did—I was, after all, always trying to smile in the face of challenges, I understood what he meant. I blamed others for the failure of things when I should have realized I should have taken half the blame. At least. In my mind, I was whole and healed, but in reality, I was still very angry, including with myself. My poor choices, my lack of letting go, and my belief in things that weren't true.

I didn't see him again. But I was thankful to have met him because he forced me to face the inner demons I'd refused to acknowledge in the past.

However, none of this had stopped me from dating. I persevered. I moved on to the next one. And the next. Too short. Too closed-minded. Too something. It was always wrong. As long as I dated, I wouldn't have to deal with the pain, nor accept the fact that I'd loved someone too much and he'd never loved me back. Easier to hope things would change and to believe the only reason we weren't together was that he was a coward. Easier than thinking he simply didn't love me.

Shortly after moving into my new place in the quiet of the country, I regretted my decision. It was too quiet, and the loneliness and boredom started to overtake me. I was writing and focusing on understanding why I was still stuck in the past, which took my mind off my solitude. I had deeply wanted solitude, but now that it was here, I felt I had made a mistake. I told myself I rarely made mistakes, except in love, so I was confused by this feeling of failure. I thought if this was supposed to be a gift from the Universe, my cottage of solitude, why then was it such a challenge? I desperately wanted a date. Anything to take my mind off what I was exploring and understanding. Don't they say to get involved in other things and get your mind off your worries and pain? Yes, maybe. But that didn't feel right to me.

I knew deep down I had to go through that and there was a reason I felt I'd made a mistake. It was uncomfortable. It was necessary. I had avoided releasing hope. I had avoided accepting that the love had only flowed in one direction. And during my time as a hermit, I learned to release hope. And I accepted that he was only being kind. He hadn't wanted to hurt me, and that's why he'd kept me hanging on energetically and physically. He'd felt guilty because he'd caused me pain, and I'd embraced his guilt by clearly telling him how much pain he had caused me. Even when I forgave him, even when I'd told him I loved him unconditionally, I was simply keeping him attached because of his guilt. I hadn't listened when he'd told me he wasn't in love with me. I'd thought he was lying or confused or in denial. But I'd been the one who'd been lying to myself and had continued to deny that it was over.

I'd even questioned my love for him. Had I loved him? There were moments when I felt it. Moments when I'd even thought he loved me. I'd thought I felt it. I'd been so sure. Again, illusion. Most of the time there was conflict, anxiety, and deep emotional discussions that kept us going in circles. I'd thought those discussions were important and had shown how much he trusted me. But I think I was simply his therapist. He'd talked and I listened. I'd helped him. I could heal him. He'd held on because I was helping. With what, I don't know. I'd been caught in confusion. Desperate. Stuck in a codependent emotional web.

So many thoughts and so many realizations. This hermit mode sucked, but it was also eye-opening. Facing the things I feared the most, I was slowly accepting everything I had denied from the very beginning. I started writing. Insanely. Non-stop, once the realizations started. But I was still angry. Not at him. I had forgiven him. I was angry at myself for being a fool. It was very hard to forgive myself for the things I'd done and the words I'd spoken. For the false beliefs I'd carried with me for far too long. *I should have known better. I'm smart.* I should have been aware of what was happening.

I know I'm not the only person this has ever happened to. Take one look at YouTube and the vast number of followers of tarot readers performing love readings. So many broken people with broken hearts who still have faith, even after ten years, that someone from their past will finally wake up and speed forward toward them to express their love. I wanted to slap them, wake them up from the illusions. *Stop hoping.* It's one thing to hope that you find love, but quite another to hope that a specific person will find their love for you. *Free will, people.* You cannot control the actions of others, and neither can the Universe. Continuing to hope and pray that someone will express their love and sweep you off your feet, no matter how "meant to be" it felt, was just another way to avoid dealing with the pain and acceptance of loss. I think the only reason I was so frustrated with those people was that I was one of them.

I'd wasted my time hoping and praying for him to come back. I should have prayed for world peace (or is that something else we can't control?). I should have prayed for inner peace and emotional healing. I should have hoped exclusively for a beautiful future without him. Such a waste of hope and prayers. I hated being wrong. *But it had felt so right.*

I even questioned my decision to break up with Alan. Maybe I should have stayed with him. I would have had a stable, secure future. I could have married him. I could've had a balanced life, fun, and adventure. *Devoid of love.* I couldn't do that, and I'm glad I came to my senses before it got too serious. Maybe my non-negotiable list should be one word—*love.*

With all these thoughts and emotions—I wanted desperately to escape solitude. But I held strong. *I'm not leaving until I'm healed or dead. And I finish my book.* I needed to finish my book before I died. So, after all, there was a reason for my little cottage and being too far from everything.

I SHOULD BE DEAD

Time passed quickly. I realized my diagnosis had been almost a year ago. Not that I didn't think about my death—I did, but it was without worry. At least for myself. I was mostly sad for those whom I would leave behind. They would suffer my loss. Or maybe they wouldn't care. No. That was a silly thought. They would care—those whom I loved and who loved me in return. I wondered if I should tell anyone. In some ways, it was unfair to them, keeping them in the dark. The sudden news of my demise would be a shock. I decided to let it go, for now.

This whole time, I mostly tried to push it out of my head. I was good at that sometimes. I could ignore my own death while obsessing about romantic love, as if it were the most important thing in life. It was easy to ignore because I wasn't feeling sick. I felt completely healthy. The doctor had told me I had about one year, but it could possibly be more than one year. I hadn't been for an appointment because I was just letting things happen. Maybe it was time to get checked. Part of me didn't want to know because I was feeling so good. Yet something seemed off, but not in a bad way. I felt healthy and strong, at least physically. The emotional part of me was a mess, but I accepted that. That was normal.

I had some scans and tests and then went to meet with the doctor. They don't tell you the results right away—you have to wait and talk to your doctor in person. So while everyone else in the medical world knows whether you will live or die, you, the victim, have to wait patiently to hear the results. I was waiting for her to tell me that the tumor was bigger and soon I would start to feel worse. I didn't expect to live. I had come to terms with everything and I saw no way to fight my death. I would become stardust—limitless, magical light.

The doctor walked in, a serious look on her face.

"I'm not quite sure how to tell you this…" she hesitated. *Here it comes.*

"Your cancer is gone."

What? I was shocked. I had prepared myself for death. I'd accepted it. I was one hundred percent ready for whatever was beyond the physical world. No fear. *And now, she tells me I'm not dying?*

"Wait. Are you sure?" I asked. "Maybe it's a mistake."

"No mistake. I hate to use the word miracle, but you're inexplicably healed," she said.

I couldn't decide if I was happy or sad. That's a strange way to feel. I should have been happy immediately, but I had already made up my mind that I was dying and had mentally prepared myself. I hated a change of plans and a change of the vision I had seen for the future.

I wasn't sure how this would change things for me. I wanted to stay balanced and single and continue my solitary, hermetic life. I needed to finish my book. I didn't want that news to change anything. *It doesn't have to change anything.*

I decided to continue just as before. No longer dying would just give me more time to finish my book. I had given up on the quest for the perfect man. It was unrealistic and harmful to my soul. I was fine without a man. I felt balanced, the same balance I'd had before, the last few times I'd stopped dating. The difference this time was that I had learned a larger lesson—a man does not define who I am. He does not cure my boredom or pain. I am who I am, and I love myself. One day, maybe soon, it would happen. I would meet the right man. Probably when I least expected it. I wasn't waiting for it anymore or changing my life or myself to make it happen. I no longer desired things that weren't right for me just to fill the empty spaces in my soul.

I wasn't healed yet. I accepted that. I wasn't perfect. I accepted that too. I was human and would probably continue to make mistakes. But at least now I understood at a deeper level why I did the seemingly wrong things I did. Maybe I could stop myself in the future. Or maybe not. Either way, I understood what it meant to be enlightened. It wasn't just faith and trust, nor was it knowing things before they happen. It was an all-encompassing love, love of the self and love of all humans despite their faults. I realized that I'd created the mud that had buried me through my endless contradictory thoughts. The feelings were real, and my intuition was true, but my mind got in the way. This time, I crawled out of the mud through acceptance.

I understood now. I was finally at peace.

MOTIONLESS MOVEMENT

I t was hard to be still. In my quiet solitude, not accomplishing much, I felt there was little movement forward. I had kept my promise to myself about dating. It wasn't as hard as I'd expected, but sometimes I would go on dating apps and swipe for a bit, never swiping right. *Just looking,* I would tell myself. It gave me some comfort, I guess, to know it was all there if I ever chose to return. But I knew wouldn't again. One thing I did know for sure was that I would not meet my soulmate on a dating app. That was true knowing. No deep emotion attached to it, just that it would happen in the real world. I had no idea when or how, but I'd learned to trust that.

I honestly didn't know when I'd be ready to date again. I was still in hermit mode and still occasionally fighting it. At times, I still wished for him. And I still got angry at myself for doing it, but it was with a little more compassion and understanding than before. I knew we were not "meant to be." He wasn't my *one*, my only soulmate. I knew the desire I felt was the need to love myself. I knew I was as messed up as he was, and we'd both been to blame.

But that was logic, and my heart still felt love and pain. Maybe it was forever. And maybe that's what I needed to accept. The pain would lessen, and the love would stay. And both of those were okay. It was okay to love someone who didn't love me back, as long as I accepted that fact and didn't have false expectations. Or hope. *I love you, I set you free, I set myself free. You are not my last chance; you are not the only one.* I can love more than one person and I have more than one soulmate.

Love is infinite.

INNOCENT GRACE

Amid my solitude, I was offered yet another opportunity for travel. This time to Egypt, another place I'd never expected to visit. I had always been scared of terrorist acts and being caught in the crossfire. I was no longer afraid. Death didn't scare me. It was just another unexpected journey to something new and exciting.

The most profound part of my trip was a nighttime visit to the King's Chamber. I was part of a tour group, and we had private time in the Great Pyramid for meditation. This was only the second day of my arrival in Cairo, and I was tired, but I was looking forward to the experience. Always searching for mystical answers.

To get to the King's Chamber in the Great Pyramid, I had to walk up a steep incline and then go through a low, narrow passage that required me to walk hunched over. I was a little nervous that I would feel trapped and confined. I'd always thought my fear of flying was because I was in a confined space, unable to escape. I briefly imagined myself having a panic attack in the pyramid. I took in a slow, steady breath. I knew I could conquer it.

As I entered, I felt completely fine. I climbed up the walkway and through the narrow passage. I was overdressed, and it was unbearably hot. I was unable to breathe. Small, short breaths. I knew that wasn't good. I would hyperventilate. The air surrounding me was too close, and my breath suffocated me. I felt the breath of the others engulfing me as I struggled for air.

I reached the chamber, and our leader started the ceremony, letting each of us one by one take a turn in the sarcophagus during the meditation. I sat against the stone wall, hoping it would cool me down. I focused on my breath. I was sweating profusely and felt uneasy.

I couldn't focus. I couldn't breathe.

Love. Light. Peace.

I repeated the mantra in my head over and over, able to relax a bit but still unable to fall into a deep meditative state.

I became aware of everything around me. I felt and heard every small movement. Someone brushed the hair away from their face. Another touched their arm. I heard the breathing of another. And even with my eyes closed, I felt the security guard watching me. Watching us. I didn't like it. Suddenly, all I wanted was to get out of there, leave, escape. But I was afraid of judgment. This was supposed to be a positive experience, a profound mystical session in the Great Pyramid. A once-in-a-lifetime, magnificent experience.

I'm in Egypt. In the Great Pyramid. I needed to relax.

As much as I tried, I couldn't relax. When my turn came to enter the sarcophagus, I wasn't thrilled, but I wasn't nervous either. It felt routine, a task I needed to accomplish, part of the experience. I felt nothing. It was expected of me, and I did my duty. I laid there, trying to feel mystical energy, divine love, and meditative peace.

Nothing. I felt nothing.

I exited and took a spot on the floor, closing my eyes, and again tried to force myself into a deep state of nirvana. It was pointless. I wanted out. I didn't want to be there, I felt uncomfortable. I didn't want to be surrounded by so many energies. Everyone around me looked as if they were in bliss. My uncomfortableness was overwhelming.

I stood up slowly, pretending I was in control and had made a rational decision to leave. I walked out without looking back. I didn't know if anyone saw me leave. I didn't know if anyone wondered why I left that highly-anticipated ceremony. I didn't care. I needed to get out.

As I made my way through the narrow passage and back down the steeply sloped stairs, I started to breathe easier. I felt lighter. I felt relief. And then, when I finally saw the night sky through the doorway, I knew I was free.

On the steps just outside the entrance to the pyramid, I felt liberated. I didn't know from what, though. It wasn't the confined space that had bothered me. I wasn't claustrophobic. I intuitively knew it had to be something deeper than that. There was something about breathing the fresh air, taking in the night sky full of stars, that made me feel love. It was beautiful. This was my profoundly positive, mystical experience. I didn't understand why or what had prompted me to leave the pyramid. All I knew was that I was truly happy being outside.

I sat on the steps. It was dark and the moon was full. I was alone and free in an ancient place full of mystery. *I am in Egypt*. It was almost as if I didn't believe I was there. It was a dream. My dream was not to be in the pyramid but to experience the grandeur and majesty from the outside.

On the outside looking in is a much better view. You see the whole picture. You look at everything from a wider perspective, a higher perspective. I could see more clearly taking in the whole picture rather than focusing on myself. I was part of the collective but had focused only on myself.

The freedom I longed for was to see everything at once—not the small details. They don't matter. How I fit into the Universe, into the fabric of time was more important.

I knew what gave me joy and deep experiences. It was the forest, not the trees. And there's nothing wrong with that. I had forced myself to examine all the details of everything I had ever done, all the choices I had made. All the branches, all the twigs, every little leaf. All my mistakes. Over and over until I was confused about what I stood for. But when I soared above and looked at the whole, I saw the strength of the connections in each choice I'd made. Together, the trees formed a canopy of wisdom and knowledge, protecting the sacred love that lived inside me.

I'd made my choice. Others might not understand, but my choice was profound to me. Instead of feeling as if I had given up and run away from the fears I should be facing, I felt free and as if a part of me had been healed. I wasn't weak in deciding to leave the space. I didn't need strength to face my fears. What I needed was the strength to make choices that empowered me. The fears were faced regardless. I chose freedom from having to do everything the way I thought it was supposed to be done. I didn't care what anyone thought. I made the intuitive choice to save myself instead of being forever trapped in someone else's vision of spirituality.

It's okay to be afraid. It's okay to be off balance. And it's okay not to do something that everyone considers highly spiritual. I'd been afraid my fears would define me and make me less than others. After all, it seemed to me that being spiritual meant being balanced and not needing meds to fly because I had meditation and my inner strength.

We're human. We have weaknesses. We have faults. Even those we see as gurus and spiritual leaders aren't perfect. They also fear. Openly admitting my fear was my true strength.

Spirituality cannot be defined by others. You need to follow your own heart and your definition of what it means to be spiritual and how you want to practice your beliefs. Spirituality doesn't mean you have to take life so seriously. You can make jokes about spirituality. You can laugh and make fun of those silly things you and others do. Taking everything too seriously takes the joy out of life. There is no guidebook. In my opinion, there are only three rules: be kind, compassionate, and exude love. Beyond that, you create your own beliefs. If you don't feel comfortable doing something that "everyone" considers spiritual, then don't do it. Take back your power and make your own choices.

Later, as I sat at the airport waiting for my flight home, I simply understood that I no longer needed my Xanax to fly. I had been taking it for almost twenty years. I couldn't get on a plane without it. I would begin to panic twenty-four hours before a flight and continue in a panicked state throughout the entire flight until I finally landed at my destination. I gripped the armrests and pleaded for the plane to stay in the air. I wasn't afraid of death—I was afraid of falling, being trapped, being unable to escape. It was uncontrollable. Sweaty palms, shortness of breath, unreasonable fear.

Something happened in Egypt that I didn't understand. At first, it didn't make sense, that I'd healed from the fear of being trapped by walking away from it and not by facing it. That's not how I understood things to work. Face your demons, face your fears, walk through the darkness—I had been through all of that, forcing myself to do the difficult things. By this reasoning, I should've stayed in the pyramid. Maybe it was about having free will. You can escape those things that make you feel trapped. You have the power to change your life.

WHAT GOES AROUND

I was one with myself and the Universe. My emotions were balanced, and my mind was clear. They were working together in perfect harmony. One did not overpower the other, nor was there a constant high-speed, round-and-round conversation between the two. Mostly. I was still learning to trust my heart and disregard the dark thoughts. My mind was the culprit that started the endless circular arguments. My emotions were the truth. Feelings of joy or sorrow don't lie. But my thoughts could very easily deceive me. My mind was my biggest enemy.

I learned to ask my heart for advice before letting my head talk. It didn't mean I automatically followed my emotions. I had to be aware of the overpowering ones and the reasons behind their manifestations. But it was an easy balance. Of course, I hadn't thrown men into the equation yet. I wasn't ready for that. The thought of it made me nervous, even though I understood where the emotions were coming from. It was easy to understand. The hard part was putting everything into practice.

I still had dreams and visions during meditation. And yes, *he* still appeared—quite frequently. But it didn't worry me. I just accepted it. When I had a dream where he was front and center, I would check my feelings first. Sometimes they were quiet and subdued, which was foreign to me. I almost didn't trust the feelings. The past had been inundated with emotion.

The more intense the emotions, the more I trusted they were true. I felt as if I was reading a book about someone else's life. Distanced. The tears or the laughter were almost emphathetic reactions to another person's story. *Those emotions don't feel like mine.* Much easier to process when I distanced myself. Much easier when the emotions weren't so intense. I had spent my life in intensity, one extreme to the other, thinking my ability to feel deeply was a beautiful thing.

He started appearing in my dreams almost nightly. I had become used to it, and it was a normal part of my life. In the beginning, I was mostly confused, and I tried to analyze the meaning of the dreams. It wasn't painful, like some of the other dreams I used to have about him where he would abandon me or some tragic circumstance would keep us apart. Just a lingering longing to have him come back, to go back to dreaming. Eventually, when I stopped thinking about the why, it became routine. Once I accepted his fifth-dimensional self in the subconscious dream state, everything just flowed. I would fall asleep, and there he was, waiting for me. We'd talk for a long while. Or sometimes go on dream adventures. I had an entire other life while I slept. It felt as if I was there for days. Sometimes there was physical affection but never sex. This was a soul expression and the physical seemed meaningless.

It was the ideal substitute for dating. But it was more than that. This was the perfect expression of my dream man, the only one I'd ever wanted. I woke up refreshed and happy.

I noticed I was sleeping more deeply and longer. I was once a six-hour-a-night sleeper, but now, I would sleep for nine-ten hours a night. I was still living a real life in the real world. Social things, work, writing. It seemed it was a good balance of sleeping and dreaming and waking and living.

One night, as we were sitting on the sand, talking about time, and whether it was linear, he asked me a question. I thought I would answer yes to that question, but I hesitated.

"Would you like to stay here forever?" he asked.

Forever was a very long time. I still had connections in real life, I still had things I wanted to do.

I answered honestly.

"I don't know."

He smiled.

"What would it mean to stay here forever? Would I be sleeping, my body still on earth?" I asked.

I imagined being on life support or in a coma. *No.* I didn't want that. Too much pain for those I love. I would never want to be on life support. I would prefer to be released to death.

"You would have to die," he replied.

So I was almost dying, then I wasn't, and now he's telling me I need to die?

"I don't want to choose to die. I want it to be natural," I said. "Can't we just continue to meet in dreams?" I hoped the answer would be yes.

He touched my hand. He didn't reply. *Was that a no?* I was hoping it wasn't.

I never asked why or how this was happening. I simply decided to accept it. I had always asked too many demanding questions of the Universe and him, but now I felt I needed to get more information. There were many things I could flow with, but this was too—final. I thought I knew what my decision would be, whether to stay with him or go back to the real world, but now I wasn't sure anymore.

"Can I ask you some questions first?" I asked, hesitantly.

He still hadn't replied to my earlier question.

"Of course," he answered. "Anything."

I took a deep breath, and asked, "Where's your body? Are you dreaming too?"

"We are all dreamers," he replied.

I shook my head.

"Please don't answer in riddles or philosophical replies. I don't understand how we are connecting. I'm dreaming, I know that. But are you real? Or are you a figment of my dream state?"

I knew I was asking too many questions at once.

"I'm sorry. I...I...I don't know what's real anymore. This, this, seems crazy. But I believe in everything, and I believe this is real, as real as dreams can be, anyway," I said.

He took my hand and said, "It's better if I show you."

We were suddenly whisked away, flying in a golden chariot across the sky.

"I am the Alpha and the Omega," he said.

My old dream of the golden chariot. We flew by all the familiar places from my dream. *Why was I dreaming this?*

When we reached the concrete slab where I had seen his body and desperately wanted to stop, it was empty.

"Where did you go?" I asked.

"I'm right here next to you!" he laughed.

Then he started spitting out numbers, the same numbers of which I had dreamt several years ago.

"Twelve, fifteen, eighteen, twenty, twenty-two. And three," he rapidly recited.

1+2=3

1+5=6

1+8=9

2022

3

The rest was all telepathy. I had done those same calculations myself. I had spent countless hours trying to solve the mystery of the numbers. I knew about the three, six, and nine—the Tesla numbers and sacred geometry. But I hadn't put 2022 together as a year. It seemed too far in the future. And I was impatient back then, wanting everything to happen immediately. I couldn't imagine why I needed to wait until 2022. I still didn't have a complete picture, though. Yes, it was 2022 and I had sacred numbers, I just didn't know how to put them all together. And that extra number three—that was puzzling.

"Why does any of this matter?" I asked.

"That's the answer to your questions," he replied.

Then, the scene around me started to dissolve, and I was slowly brought back to the waking world.

Normally, I would have been upset to leave things hanging, but there was something I needed to do in the waking world.

I looked up to the sky and said with conviction, "I'll see you later."

I knew he'd be there.

MYSTERIES OF
THE UNIVERSE

I jumped out of bed and gathered all my journals, every notebook, and all the loose notes I had lying all over the house. I needed to look through everything. Not just for those numbers, but for other numbers. Words I had seen in dreams and visions. Look at them numerically. I probably could've just made everything appear in my dream, but this was more concrete, more solid. I was a little hesitant to trust the dream world right now. I was too comfortable there. And was he himself? Was he, and were the dreams, just my creation? There was a connection. And it had to be in my notes.

Not knowing exactly where to start, I first read every entry from March (the third month), June (the sixth month), and September (the ninth month). There was too much, so I narrowed it doing again, to the third, sixth, and ninth days of those months. I read quickly. I went through every entry for those days for the year of my journals since I'd started dreaming about the numbers. There were some significant things, but I wasn't sure how they all fit together. Plus, maybe 12, 15, and 18 were the correct numbers. And what about the number three? I also found at one point, that if I took the first numbers and divided them by three, I got four, five, and six. You couldn't divide 20 or 22 by three, so I became stuck. Unless I divided only the first three numbers by three. Three kept repeating. It was all unknown. I tried another strategy.

I assembled the items I'd been given on my travels: the stone, the pendant, and the coin. I thought about how they could connect to the numbers. Well, there were three items, given to me by three people, in three different places. Kansas, Colorado, and Peru. Nothing significant there. A bear pendant, a golden coin, and a green, heart-shaped stone. I picked up each item and focused my energy on it. The bear pendant was hand-carved by my mysterious disappearing mountain man. The meaning of that encounter, well, was it about conquering my fears? I'd also had several dreams about a bear. The stone was about love and keeping my heart open. It looked like serpentine. *I need to look up the meaning of serpentine.* The message was clear about the stone. I needed to search for anything in my journals about stones.

And finally, the coin. Flip a coin, make a decision? I picked it up. That's when I noticed, the words on the coin had changed *again*. This time, the words said: *What you seek, can be found in dreams.*

What did that mean? That I should go back to my dream? I needed to finish looking at my journals first. I decided to put both the stone and coin in my pocket and put the bear pendant around my neck. Maybe they would energetically tell me something.

So much to decipher. It was overwhelming, and I still didn't have any answers. Just more questions. No—I had answers, I just didn't know what questions were being asked. *Still.* The only thing I was sure about was the year 2022. I knew in my gut the year was significant.

But why?

THE NUMBERS

Journal Entry

I was walking down an old seaside street. There were shops and restaurants along the water. Suddenly, a door opened, and a man came out and looked me straight in the eye.

He said, "Remember these numbers: 12, 15, 18, 20, 22."

Then he shut the door. A few seconds later, he opened the door again and said, "And the number three. Don't forget the numbers."

That was it. All he said.

I'm not sure what they mean. Are they dates? Significant years of my life? They look like dates and times. December 15, 2018. And the number three could be what? Three years? Three years from December 15, 2018? What will happen on that date?

I can assign letters to the numbers. Maybe they will spell a word. C, L, O, R, T, V. They spell nothing that makes any sense. Another O and I could have color TV. What the heck does that mean? Even if I mix them up and turn them around, I still have nothing. They all add up to nine if I keep adding them together to create a single digit. I need to look up the meaning of the number nine.

Check longitudes, latitudes, Bible verses, division by three, musical notes, sacred geometry, and math patterns. Roman numerals? Numerology and sacred numbers? Periodic table?

THE RABBIT HOLE

I spent the afternoon looking for answers. Bears, stones, and coins, and trying to decipher and connect the meaning of the numbers to my objects. I dreamt about tigers more than I did about bears, and they were all very powerful dreams. I also dreamt about a golden lion.

Lions and tigers and bears, oh my.

Predators. Fears. I collected stones from every place I went. The green heart stone had been given to me, though. I knew they were important. I also had dreamt about other numbers. More to add to the mix.

In one method, assigning letters to numbers and combining yet more incoming numbers I got the word Covid. C = 3, derived from 12 (1+2=3); etc. Maybe I'd predicted Covid in my dream? That was too much. *I'm not that kind of psychic.* Plus, the future wasn't predictable. Luxor. I'd gone to Luxor, Egypt, in 2022. I'd also gone to Peru, but the numbers didn't spell that at all. I pulled out other numbers I had dreamt about. Earth? Covid earth? Love. Light. So many possibilities, but they all felt random. I thought maybe the answers would come with time. But the end of 2022 was quickly approaching, and I was afraid I wouldn't have answers until 2023. Maybe the numbers weren't important at all. Just a random or a false mystery to keep me occupied, perhaps meant to keep me out of trouble. *Well, that didn't work, did it.* I guess it's difficult to protect yourself *from* yourself.

Maybe that's the point. Wait and see. *Not yet.*

I felt I was missing something important. It was probably something simple that connected everything, including my current dreams. There was just too much information to sort through. I decided to wait until sleep and hope the answer would come to me in my dreams. The only thing I knew was that I didn't want to sleep forever.

WE CREATE OUR REALITY

I remember a conversation he and I once had in dreamland. I couldn't think of a better name for my dream state, so it became officially dreamland.

At one point, I wondered if the stories I wrote would come true. Because I wrote an independent, strong ending for my character, did that mean I would also be alone? If I wrote that one character abandoned the other, would that happen to me in real life? We create our reality, but I think I was pushing that idea too far. Maybe I created other realities, not mine. Maybe they were alternate universes or timelines, past or future lives. Maybe the human before me had created my reality, and I was creating the reality of the next future human "me." Lots to think about.

I asked him about this. He said he didn't know for sure, but he thought that maybe the dream world was the reality, and what we experienced in our day-to-day existence was a state of sleep. We were, after all, mostly going through the physical motions of living but were not really alive. I understood what he meant. And while many other spiritual souls would also understand, I thought most of the "waking" world was sound asleep and wouldn't understand. Humans like to classify their singular life in general ways as if their one life is the entire scope of their existence. Humans believe their lives are beautiful, horrible, traumatic, perfect, etc. Maybe their past selves created this world for them for whatever reason. Some say it's to grow, learn, and evolve. Perhaps the more challenging lives are created by the ones who have learned enough to deal with the horribleness of human existence. Those who suffer in their lifetime…well, I don't know. I'd like to think the terrible things in the world happen for a reason. Because if I were God, I wouldn't let them happen. Perhaps it's just simply the humans who create the terribleness for others. God can guide us, but she has no power to affect human choices. Then we would jump into a discussion of free will vs. destiny.

This would continue for several hours. It was paradise for me, the great seeker of knowledge and the answers to all the *whys* of life. I didn't necessarily think he knew everything, but he brought up so many good points, I believed everything he said was true. I wasn't quite sure how the man who'd seemed so lost had ended up being my guide.

Never say never.

TO SLEEP,
PERCHANCE TO DREAM

It was still early, but I was tired. I spent too many hours poring over notes as well as researching online. I didn't think I'd found anything new, just more possibilities that weren't definitive. My head felt heavy. Too much thinking today. I'd love to just dream of sleep tonight instead of more philosophies and riddles.

I picked up my book and read for a bit until I felt the tiredness creep in. For some reason, I wasn't as excited about our meeting tonight.

Why? Maybe because I thought I would have to decide. *Dream forever or not at all.* It sounded as if he'd said that—hadn't it? I wasn't sure.

This is my dream. I can control it. But I knew this was no ordinary dream. It was something created by the two of us, and we controlled it together. A collaborative dream. I couldn't make the decision alone. We would have to agree. And that's why he'd asked me if I wanted to stay there forever. I wasn't even sure how I knew all this, but it probably came from my higher self.

I'm so casual and matter-of-fact about so many things. *Oh, just another vision, just another dream lover.* I had accepted miracles as everyday occurrences.

I hadn't realized I had fallen asleep until I saw the oasis

in the middle of a beautiful desert. I could see a tent, a small stream, and some palm trees. And him. He was outside the tent waving me toward him. He was always there before me, waiting. I don't remember ever arriving before him. It was all familiar. He often picked the desert when it was his turn to choose. For some reason, he loved the desert. I preferred the sand on a beach with an ocean more than an expanse of desert. But I could see the beauty.

"Hi," he said as he took my hand and led me to a chair.

I was a little nervous. Usually, our gatherings were unplanned, but this one felt purposeful because I had so many questions. I knew what I wanted, what I had wanted for a long time, but I wasn't sure what I would be giving up in return. I knew to gain something I would have to surrender something in exchange. Balance in all things is an equal give and take. I wasn't sure I was ready to give my life despite the love I felt for him.

It's all a dream.

He grabbed an apple from a bowl on the table and took a bite.

"Here, something for a snack," he said, tossing me one.

I held the apple, inhaling the fragrant fruity scent. I liked apples, but I was more likely to dream of eating more exotic foods. I set the apple down without biting into it.

"I have a lot of questions," I remarked a little hesitantly.

I had stopped asking why about many things, learning to accept that some things could not be answered and I had to let them go. Just flow. This was different. Flowing didn't make things feel so permanent. If I chose to stay with him, how would things flow?

He looked at me intently, prepared for what I had to say. He didn't seem fazed by my comment.

He took another bite of the apple.

"Okay, go ahead," he said.

"You know I'm happy here with you. I haven't asked any questions. But at the same time, I don't understand what all of this," I waved my hand over the landscape, stopping at him, "is."

He was silent, letting me continue.

"How are you here in my dream?" I asked. "And why does it seem so real?"

"I don't know. I don't know how it happens. I fell asleep one night, and there you were. I'm just as mystified as you," he replied.

Last night, he'd implied that he had answers. Or had that just been my interpretation? He was accepting of everything without question. I'd also been, until last night, when he'd asked me to stay. Maybe he hadn't understood what he was asking.

"How do I know if you're real?" I asked. "Why are we not together in real life?"

The question came out before I had time to stop it. I hadn't wanted to ask that question. It would bring everything crashing down to earth, back to reality. In my gut, I already knew the answer to that.

He ran both hands through his hair and rested his hands on top of his head.

"Well," he started, "I don't know with one hundred percent certainty if this is real if you're real. I'm happy here with you, and I just thought maybe we could just stay here. I don't even know if it's possible. But I want it."

He paused.

"As for your other question, why aren't we together in real life, you know the answer to that. We're not ready. At least not now."

Not now. Not yet. Inconclusive answers.

Time in the real world was advancing. Soon we would be too old. The *not now* likely meant another lifetime. Even if time wasn't linear, as humans we feel it as such, and I was still hoping for some sort of romance in the waking world. I wasn't desperate or looking, but companionship and adventure were always a possibility.

Was dreaming enough?

"What does staying here forever mean?" I asked. "Will I be sleeping forever? Will I be dead? Those things matter. I don't want my family to suffer if I'm in a coma or something for the rest of my life."

I don't know what made me think he had the answers to these questions. Like me, he didn't understand how and why we were together here.

"This is what I think. Time doesn't flow the way we think. Right now, back on earth, or reality, or whatever you want to call it, time has slowed. It hasn't stopped, but it's always flowing. While we're here together, it's flowing at a different speed."

He paused, then started again. "Wait, that doesn't make sense. It's hard for us to understand because we only perceive time as linear. You don't have to be asleep to experience this dream. You are experiencing it regardless. It's happening simultaneously as you are living your daily life. There are an infinite number of you, each doing different things, none the same. Many timelines, many universes, however you want to perceive it. Everything happens simultaneously. The past is now, the future is now. We are living all at once."

"I understand that. But it seems the longer I'm here, the more time passes in the waking world. I sleep longer. I don't want to sleep forever."

"Do you sleep longer? How do you know that you aren't awake now and are sleeping when you're awake? Which world is the real world?" he asked.

I had asked myself those questions at times. But there was no way I could ever answer them. *Not yet*. How could I decide without knowing the truth? I wasn't even going to ask that question. That would lead to a deep discussion of the meaning of truth.

Maybe this wasn't real. Perhaps I was just having discussions with myself. I created him. This was my dream, created for comfort or companionship. Maybe he is the Universe, helping me find answers. God was speaking to me through him. The thoughts didn't worry me. I was fine with whatever the answer was—I just wanted to know.

"We are the Universe," he replied, reading my thoughts. "I understand why you're hesitant. If you're asleep, does the real world exist?"

Schrödinger's Cat. I knew what he meant. Maybe. We are simultaneously awake and asleep. And what box would need to be opened? Too much to think about. I wanted concrete answers.

"So are you saying if I stay here, I would still be awake in the real world?" I asked.

"Or asleep in the dream world," he replied.

This was unproductive. We could talk in circles for hours, and I still wouldn't know the truth. The real, waking truth.

"I need some more time," I said. "But before I go, I want you to know something. I'm sorry for everything I did. Sorry for pressuring you, and sorry for wanting to move everything so quickly. I was really scared. I felt the fear. It turned into worry and anxiety about everything. I didn't want to tell you because I was afraid it would add to your fear, and I felt I was being a hypocrite. Telling you to jump in while I was fearful. I know you tried. But I was too scared. I had to let you go. I didn't have any real hope, although I always said I did. I was adamant about it. Hope is tricky. I saw the reality and the way you withheld information. How could I trust you? In the end, I didn't. We were two fearful people trying to make something happen. It never could have worked. You were right when you said it was the wrong time."

He tried to stop me, but I had more to say.

"I wasn't happy," I continued. "I could never admit that to myself. I needed to find *my* happiness. Alone. I didn't see that then. I was so afraid of letting you go, because with you I was happy, and I felt like I was home. I can't describe it any other way. I think I knew in my heart we weren't ready—at least, I wasn't ready. But I desperately wanted it and pushed so hard."

"I know all that," he replied. "And it's okay. I forgive you."

"I wanted you to know all of this, just in case," I said.

He said nothing else. I don't ever recall telling him that, but I was sure he could read my mind. I wasn't even sure apologies in dreams counted. It was the best I could do. I could hope that somehow his waking self would get the message, and that it would give him peace and release him from any pain or guilt.

I wasn't even sure I trusted the dream anymore. I didn't trust he was real. I didn't trust myself to make a decision. Not now. I was still healing and wasn't ready to give up anything for something so tenuous.

I stood and stated, "I'll be back."

"I'll be there," he replied.

There? Did he mean here?

The dream faded and was back in my bed. It was 3:33 a.m. I was tired but afraid to go back to sleep, afraid of being pulled back into a dream with him. I needed to find my answers elsewhere.

I debated reaching out to him in the real world and asking him all those questions, but I wasn't sure his waking self would even remember what was happening in his dreams. I felt I was interacting with his higher self, and his earthbound self was unaware. *Too risky.* I had to leave him be.

I opted for more sleep, willing myself not to return to our dream. I needed to dream alone.

LIFE HACK

Journal Entry

I dreamt I was in front of a computer, playing a game called Life. It wasn't the game I remembered from childhood and was very similar to *The Sims* computer game. I grew bored quickly. It was the same thing over and over, and every time I tried to change things or make a different choice, everything moved too slowly. I chose an option, I can't remember what, and I waited. Five minutes. Then ten. Hours later, nothing had happened. Maybe the game had been corrupted? I noticed a countdown clock on the screen. It was hardly moving. What seemed like an hour to me was only a second in my dream.

Someone handed me a hack code. It would auto-play the game and speed things up. I didn't want to cheat but was too impatient to wait. I could do other things while Life played on. I typed in the code. The computer accepted it and the screen started blinking. The blinking came faster and faster until the computer completely turned off. I'd broken the game—maybe the whole system?

Then, just as suddenly as it had turned off, it roared back to life, numbers and words scrolling by too fast to read. An analog clock appeared on the screen, and the hands were speedily spiraling in opposite directions, completely out of control. Time moved forward and backward too fast. My own life ended, and then I was born again in the same life, reliving the same events over and over.

I tried to regain control of the game and delete my hack code, but I'd been locked out. Time was spinning out of control and was forever stuck in a loop. *Maybe I can just turn off the computer.*

I pushed the power button. Nothing happened. I pulled the plug from the wall. The computer wasn't turning off. There was nothing I could do. I was helpless.

THE AWAKENING

I understood the meaning of the dream—you can't control many things in life, and if you try to, you only make things worse. But what was my hack now? Was dreaming with him my cheat? Was I trying to escape something I needed to face?

I had no idea what I was supposed to face. I had accepted many things and had healed a lot. I knew healing never ended. Healing was life, life was healing.

The answer to my dilemma wasn't in words of advice or philosophy. It was in me. The meaning of things could only be interpreted by me. The signs, the visions, and the synchronicities all came from my higher, wiser self, imparting advice and wisdom to lead me on my path. The search for meaning wasn't necessary.

The bear pendant was to remind me to be courageous and that I was protected. The stone, to open my heart to love. And the coin reminded me that there was always a flip side to everything. Good and bad, duality. And I wouldn't necessarily know which side was good. There were no good or bad choices. I just had to make them without thinking too much.

A leap of faith.

I already knew the answers to many things subconsciously. I had to trust that my higher self and my waking self were integrated enough to understand the meanings.

And there were things I didn't know or couldn't know. Not yet. Though *not yet* wasn't really predictable, eventually, all my answers would come. And that's when I knew what I wanted to do.

I wasn't ready to sleep. I'd been asleep for too much of my life. I wanted to be awake and live every moment. Whether I was with him or not would not be the biggest deciding factor. I knew I would see him again one day, whether in this life or the next, even if I abandoned the dream. I knew in my heart this was true.

I wanted to say goodbye but wasn't sure it was necessary. I was certain we were connecting all the time on a higher plane. He would know. So I decided I wouldn't dream that same old dream but rather would dream only about new things. New dreams I hadn't dreamt before, new possibilities. I intuitively knew I had the power to make that change.

"I love you," I whispered.

It was done.

GRATITUDE

I finally finished the first draft of my book on December 12. I still had a lot of editing to do. In the meantime, I set up my writing workshops again after a three-year hiatus. I wanted to connect with new people. I had no desire to date. I would find someone when the time was right. I was at peace, and he no longer appeared in my dreams. Although part of me still wondered if I would find the meaning behind the numbers before the end of 2022, I wasn't obsessed anymore, nor was I waiting for events to happen. I was in a state of gratitude.

I knew the moments of joy in my past outshone the moments of confusion, but I had focused on the pain. In my journals, there was more positivity than negative thinking. I focused on the pain narrative because that's what would ultimately give me healing. I was always able to find the beauty of nature. I loved sunrises and sunsets, the water, stormy days, and clear starlit nights. Pictures—I took pictures of everything. Even though those images were in my head, the pictures reminded me of the awesomeness of nature, and that it would always be there, something to look forward to every day. I loved my long walks along the river, my time for quiet contemplation. It removed me from being in my head about everything. Perhaps I was more balanced in the past than I'd first perceived.

I was grateful for the food I ate. I relished the flavors of food, the experience of cooking and creating something delicious. I became a cook again in my solitude. Adding spices and flavor and experimenting with all sorts of recipes. Changing them made everything taste better. It wasn't just for sustenance—food was an experience, an almost orgasmic bliss of sensations. I savored every moment of eating.

I was in my element while traveling, experiencing new cultures, and learning the history of mystical places. The newness of each experience gave me such peace, as well as a recognition that there was so much more to life than trying to find a perfect man. But sometimes in those moments of pure joy, where I expected that I would cut loose those desires for a man, I would be sad because I didn't have a companion to share those beautiful moments. It wasn't about having someone there to make me feel better—it was about the shared experience. It was the beauty of the moment—the desire to share it with someone. Yet I didn't really like that feeling. It made me feel as if I should be grateful for what I already had, and it was too much to ask for. I fought it sometimes, thinking it wasn't normal. I'd read so many books, articles, and too many things on the internet about how I should be happy and grateful. The moment I started wanting something else to be added to my experience, it was somehow wrong because it ruined my gratitude.

Be happy for what you have, I would tell myself. While I was, there were moments when I missed a relationship. I knew it was completely okay to feel this way, but I fought with myself about it sometimes. Not as intensely as I'd done in the past. Rather, it was a quiet disagreement. I was trying to prove I was healed, and to heal meant letting go of my desires for a man. It took me a long time to accept that it was a normal feeling.

That had been my problem. I had constantly judged my feelings as being right or wrong. I wanted to do everything *right*. I didn't exactly know why, perhaps just to prove to myself and others that I was whole, and wholeness meant not wanting anything and being grateful for what I already had. But it's a human condition to want. It has to be accepted. The important part was understanding why I wanted something so badly and deciding whether it would complement my life or simply fill a void.

I already have my cake, and a man is just the icing. That's probably why I treated men with such contempt. Why couldn't I just mix him into the batter? Because there were so many failures in dating and relationships, I decided they would sour the flavor of the cake. This was my cake, and it gave me the bliss I needed. The icing could wait.

It was empowering in many ways to realize I didn't need them. I was content on my own.

You can't have true happiness until you find that joy alone. If you're always searching for the perfect man to make you happy, you will always fail. Only you can make yourself happy. And that takes a lot of work.

The joy I found in my hermithood was real. Yes, there were days of loneliness, but they were rare. Sometimes it would come when the character in my book needed to go through something difficult. I embodied her. Her fiction became my life. But I didn't stop writing, because it helped my character become more human and helped me accept many things about myself. We became entangled as I sorted through the emotions of what it meant to be a single, older woman in an insane digital dating world.

All of us, men and women alike, are broken and healing. Everyone has had different challenges, and it takes compassion, understanding, and kindness to connect with another person in a meaningful way. I lacked those in the past because I was self-absorbed. But that's the human way. We are about self first. It's all about *me* until we learn to let go of our egos. I hoped that with this new understanding, I could venture back into the dating world in the future.

I was immersed in writing my book, and I sometimes didn't want to see people. It felt like an intrusion into the world I was creating. I felt I needed solitude to work. I would be irritated by people stopping by to say hello. Even seeing friends would mean I had to stop writing. I was up and writing at three a.m. most days. That's when I felt the most inspiration. Which meant I hated going out after six p.m. Bedtime was around eight p.m. I would read and research until I fell asleep around eight-thirty p.m. At first, I wasn't looking forward to the holidays because it meant I would have to take time away from my writing, so I wrote furiously from three in the morning until I was too burnt out to write anymore. I wanted to finish before Christmas. It became extremely necessary for me.

I felt like those writers you hear about who lock themselves up for months in a cabin to finish their books. I was now one of them, even though I wasn't sure most of the time what the hell I was writing about. Or even if it was good. It wasn't a memoir. It was all fiction, yet the story I was telling touched me at such a personal level. I became my character and didn't want to share myself with anyone. It was an intrusion into my soul. I couldn't break free from my writing, at least not until my main character's journey was complete. Everyone always asked about my book, and

I only gave little snippets. I still didn't know exactly how to end the story. A happy, romantic ending sounded trite. But there was nothing wrong with being trite and cheesy. I accepted that about myself. It was only a story, but perhaps my character needed that ending, to believe in the magic of the Universe and the possibility of hope.

I didn't feel any regret about not returning to him in dreamland. I knew my future would be filled with adventure, joy, and love. Whether or not I found another man to love didn't matter to me anymore. What I wanted was the joy of living in the real world because those experiences were the ones that mattered. Dreams were beautiful, but the truth of reality was far more blissful and genuine.

CLOSURE

On December 15, just as I was finishing the final editing of my book, I received a text message from *him*. I didn't feel it was out of the blue. I wasn't surprised, which was usually how I felt when he'd reached out in the past. I wasn't nervous or anxious. It just seemed right. Normal, as if I had expected it all along. Which I had, although I didn't know the *when*. I had presumed in a future life. I was ready to move on.

It was a simple message: *Hello, was wondering how you were doing.*

This time I didn't hesitate, overthink, or strategize. I replied immediately.

Me: *I'm fine. Can I call you?*

Him: *Yes.*

It was a brief conversation. We both had too much to say that could only be said in person. We set a time to meet a few days later, on December 18 after my workshop ended. I felt…*peace*. Whatever the outcome, I knew I would be okay.

HE SPEAKS,
SOMETIME IN THE PAST

There are two sides to every story. I think you need to hear my side because I don't feel her story is a complete explanation of what happened.

When I met her, I felt the same connection she described. There was a feeling of having known her far longer. As if I already knew her. She was irresistible. Her beauty, her personality, her energy. In her presence, something peaceful and at the same time overwhelming.

I wanted to be with her, have some sort of relationship with her, but she wanted too much from me too soon. I felt as if she was trying to suck out my soul. She was too intense. I could feel it when we were together. It was as if she was forcing herself on me. I don't mean that physically. It was something in her energy, her overpowering vibe. I mean, it was beautiful, but it was too much.

I knew she loved me—even before she said it. I had my dreams or visions or whatever she called them. I knew it was coming. But I didn't love her back in the same way. Nope. Regardless of what she thought, I was not in love. I loved her as a person, but I was not in love with her. I think she was living in a fantasy world. She claimed her intuition or some mystical divine presence had guided her toward me. Well, I have my own story about that. All the signs I received pointed me away from her—very clearly.

And I followed my intuition.

I'll admit I made mistakes. I didn't behave with complete honesty, but I thought she understood. I made it very clear, always. We would never be together as a couple. She kept coming back, reaching out. I thought she wanted to be friends, and I hoped we could just be friends. It was impossible. I was connected to her, and when we were together the feelings were overwhelming. I was confused about our relationship and its intensity. I didn't know how to define it or how to understand it. I couldn't deal with her, be with her, be near her. But at the same time, she was just so damned intoxicating, and I was pulled to her like a magnet. I couldn't control myself, and for that I was sorry. I didn't want to lead her on. I didn't want to make her think I cared for her in the same way she cared about me. I wanted to keep things simple in my life. And this connection was way too complicated.

I said a lot of things I shouldn't have said, especially about the woman I was dating at the time. I regret that. I'm not sure why I told her those things because I was relatively happy with my new relationship. During one of our conversations, she asked me if I loved this other woman. She was always very direct with her questions. I was honest. I said no. It was too soon. She lectured me about continuing to date this other woman when there was no love. I didn't explain myself clearly. I didn't even know what to say. But I did say I was happy regardless of love. Happiness was important.

I decided not to contact her anymore, and some time passed by. Several months later, she sent me an insane text about how I was running away, how she had figured everything out, and how we could try to work through our differences. I didn't reply. A few weeks another text came, and she apologized for everything. Said she was over me and she had moved on. I didn't believe her. Not for one minute did I believe she was over me. I just felt it intuitively.

She's an amazingly beautiful person, but I'm over everything. Maybe it was the timing. It was both of us. I don't think I should take all the blame. Maybe we knew each other in a past life. Maybe that's why the connection was so strong. Maybe we will meet and be together in another life. But never in this one. It just can't be. Not now.

What would I say to her now? I hope you find peace. I hope love comes your way. I hope you can forgive me. I denied my love for you, yet to this day I'm not sure of my feelings. There was too much confusion. I didn't intend to add to your confusion. And I didn't mean to hurt you. In the end, maybe I just wanted a friend. But I was too broken. We both were.

HESITATION

As soon as I hung up the phone, I started to have doubts. I was willing to meet him, to at least give him closure. I felt I already had my closure. My issues with letting him go were my problems to deal with, and there was nothing he could say that would help me let go. I was concerned about rehashing the past, bringing up things that were probably better off staying buried. I'd known he would reach out, but now that it had happened, I wondered if it would benefit me to see him.

I had come so far, and I didn't want to take any more steps backward. In the past, this was all I had wished for, for him to reach out. I no longer needed that. I had pushed through my dark night of the soul, and now that I was finally in the light, that's where I wanted to stay. It would take strength and balance if I was going to see him—strength over any possible confusion in my emotions and balance to keep those emotions in check. My heart and mind needed to work together. I was confident I could accomplish the task.

UNDERSTANDING

I arrived early. Usually, he was there before me, just like in my dreams, but that day, I was there first. I was relaxed. I had no worries or expectations. I already had closure. I had already forgiven him, but I wanted to offer my apology for everything that had happened. Back then I'd been too broken to see my mistakes. I hoped he would forgive me. Maybe we both needed this meeting to move on.

I watched him arrive. He looked very different. He was thinner, and I didn't observe the same falsely confident swagger, the way he used to carry himself. His confidence now seemed authentic. His face was different, more relaxed. And his eyes were the most changed. I remembered sometimes looking into his eyes and seeing pain and confusion. But now I saw clarity. And peace.

We hugged. I still felt the connection. It was beautiful. I smiled to myself, remembering. There was no anxiety, no sadness, or regret. Just a simple feeling of love for a special soul. No romantic feelings or expectations for a relationship. I felt his love too—simple and non-romantic.

We talked about everything that had happened to us since we'd last seen each other many years ago. A lot had happened to both of us. Good and bad. We were changed but were still the same souls.

I didn't ask any questions. I let him speak. He seemed to have a lot to say.

"The first thing I want to say is I'm sorry. For everything. Whatever I said or did to hurt you. I never intended to. I was very confused, very scared, and didn't know what to make of our connection," he said.

I told him I appreciated his words. "I forgave you a long time ago. But it means a lot to hear your apology in person," I replied.

I continued, "I'm sorry, too. I was off-balance and broken. I became obsessed, desperate. I blamed you for everything. But in reality, we were both to blame. We were both in pain. I didn't see that for a long time."

He then continued.

"I've already forgiven you, too. I don't want to rehash the past. I don't know if we need to look at everything all at once. We can talk about it. But I'm here for a reason."

He paused.

"I'm sorry for walking away. I had to. I couldn't figure out a way to deal with or understand our connection. I felt it. Always. I told myself it was physical, and then later told myself it was some sort of karmic soul connection and that we needed to stay away from each other. I was broken, too. I was hurting from my heartbreak, and I wasn't ready. I shouldn't have been dating. But I was hoping to erase my heartbreak by meeting someone new. I didn't know I wasn't ready until it was too late."

Just like me trying to ease the pain by diving back into dating.

I smiled and replied, "I know. And I understand. I didn't understand for a long time. I thought that if you loved someone, you'd just jump right in without hesitation. I didn't see that I'd made wrong assumptions until I tried to enter into other relationships after you. I was scared.

Terrified. I ran away or sabotaged everything. Or I picked men who weren't right for me. I wasn't healed. I was even more broken than before, and I went around smiling and telling everyone how happy and healed I was. It took me a long time to accept that I was shattered and an even longer time to heal. Many mistakes. I've only recently found peace. I'm still healing. But I mostly understand the reasons and the lessons."

"I lied," he said.

I was about to say, *Yes, I know, and I understand,* when he said, "I did love you. I was in love with you. I am still in love with you," he stated.

I wasn't shocked. I had always known he loved me. Always. Even when I denied it to myself or was trapped in my thoughts. At every moment, I knew.

It was a knowing.

He handed me a golden coin. *Just like my coin.* On one side was a grizzly bear standing on a smooth, green, heart-shaped stone. He was looking out from the top of a mountain. In the distance, another bear made her way toward him. I flipped the coin over. On the other side was the word: *Completion.*

"Where did you find this?" I asked as I pulled my coin from my purse.

"I found it in the sand at the beach. It's not real gold, but I thought it was interesting and thought it might mean something."

"I have one, too," I said, handing him my coin.

"That's funny. They're exactly alike," he said.

I took my coin from him. He was right. The coins were exactly alike. I don't know when my coin had changed this time, but it now showed the two bears on the stone. I told him the story of my coin, the stone, and the bear pendant. There was no judgment or jealousy. He listened and accepted every word.

We sat quietly for a minute and looked at each other. The eye gaze, the exploration of the soul. We were the same, yet different.

"Do you think we can try again?" he asked, taking my hand.

I thought that if we ever had this opportunity, I would have immediately said yes, just like I thought I would have stayed in a dream forever with him.

I took just a moment, though. A small intuitive check-in. I was still healing, and I needed to make sure this felt okay.

"Yes, but we still have a lot to talk about," I replied. "This time, we take things slower," I added.

"But without fear," he replied.

"And with a little bit of hope," I answered.

We both paused.

"Can't Help Falling in Love" started playing in the background.

Everything will be okay.

"Yes," we both replied in unison.

NOT THE END

"That's a beautiful ending," he said.

"That's not the end," I said, shaking my head.

He looked surprised.

"Let me tell you the rest. We were genuinely happy for several months. It was pure bliss. Everything flowed smoothly, with open communication and many moments of love. It was everything I had hoped for.

One morning, I woke up, and he was gone. He'd completely disappeared."

"He left you," the man said.

"No, he was just gone. As if he'd never existed. His belongings, everything related to him that was in physical form just disappeared.

"When I woke up and saw he wasn't there, I thought maybe he'd run out to the grocery store or something. I texted him and didn't receive a reply. A few hours later, I grew worried. I kept calling and texting. Nothing. Then I noticed his clothes were gone. Everything connected to him was gone. His pictures were gone from my phone. And the strangest thing of all was that nobody remembered him.

I called my family and friends, and when I mentioned his name, nobody knew who he was.

Is he your new guy? Who is that?

I called one of my best friends and asked her to tell me about him. Of course, she thought I was confused. She had no idea what I was talking about. It was all very strange.

I used to joke sometimes that I had imagined him, that he was a figment of my deranged mind or a waking dream. I began to believe that this might be true. That he had never been there at all, that he had never reached out, and weren't even together in the real world. That I had fantasized about him for the last several years of my life.

Since we'd been together the last few months, my dreams had stopped. Not a single dream. Sometimes I would have a vague memory of a dream, a snippet as I moved through the day, but as soon as I tried to remember the dream or write it down, it would disappear. This was not anything I normally did. I always remembered my dreams. I had a dream journal that I'd kept for years, and it was full of dreams. Until we were together."

The man looked at me, urging me to continue.

THE MYSTERIOUS DISAPPEARANCE

By midday, it appeared as though he had never existed. I could find nothing connected to him. Not in the memories of others, not at his job. I rummaged in my drawer for the coin, the stone, and other mystical objects from my recent past. They had all disappeared. The blue bottle was gone. *My journals.* I read through them and was shocked to find there was not a word written about him— nothing about the numbers and nothing about the pain and healing over the last several years.

If he didn't exist, why was he still in my memories?

Am I dreaming?

In one of the journals, I found pages and pages of a story I didn't remember writing. It was about a woman who somehow travels to a different timeline. It's almost the same as her real world, but her lover no longer exists. It sounded familiar to what was happening to me.

Had I shifted to another timeline? But how?

Any normal person would have panicked, but I didn't. I knew there was something metaphysical involved. I just needed to solve the mystery.

I needed to get out, talk to people, explore the world around me, and try to find the truth. I thought about going back to sleep and willing myself to dream the answers, but then I thought that I may have been dreaming at that moment. Or maybe I had dreamt the entire last few years of my life. A dream within a dream…

I was looking for my keys when I found a notebook in a drawer. I opened it and saw my handwriting. There was only one entry.

LOST MEMORY

Something strange happened. I woke up but felt as if I was dreaming. I saw him lying there beside me, but he was fuzzy, like a hologram, and his body kept shifting in and out of view. Then I noticed this was happening in the entire room. I looked at my hand, but it was solid.

Not sure whether I was dreaming, I got up and found an empty notebook in the other room. I needed to write about what was happening and document what was happening. It was just a feeling.

As I'm writing, the pen no longer feels solid in my hand. Something is happening and I need to document this. I can no longer write in the past tense. I'm in the moment now, waiting for whatever will happen next...

I didn't remember writing that. Unless I'd been sleepwalking or written it while drunk. I had no recollection of it. There wasn't any back-and-forth in my mind. I must have shifted timelines overnight and somehow managed to jot down a few notes. But how and why? And how had the notebook followed me?

I needed to find answers, but I had no idea where to begin.

SOLVING THE PUZZLE

In my mind, there were several possibilities.

1. I'd been dreaming for the last few years
2. I was dreaming now
3. I'd shifted timelines
4. I was mentally ill and was having severe hallucinations

It was possible I could have dreamt everything. My dreams were sometimes so vivid that I thought they were real. It was also possible that I was dreaming at that very moment. I could also just as easily have shifted into another timeline. But that was problematic because there was no *why* or *how* that I could think of. Mental illness—very possible. Delusions and fantasies, I'd been living in my mind. However, the fact that I thought I may have been insane made it seem less likely. I hated to use the word crazy, but someone had once said only crazy people think they're not crazy. So if I think I'm crazy, then I'm not. But then again, I could be crazy and pretend I think I'm crazy.

I chose sanity, and I was pretty sure I was awake and the last few years were not a dream. He'd been mentioned in the surviving notebook, so obviously he did exist. The fact that he had disappeared was really because I had disappeared.

I was in a different place in time and space. And I had no damned idea how to get back.

IT'S TIME

I knew I wouldn't find answers here. I needed to leave. As I started toward the door, the room started spinning. I leaned against the wall for balance, thinking I was having a sudden dizzy spell. I closed my eyes for a second, and when I opened them, everything was different. I was in a pure white room with four walls, no windows, and one door. I was no longer in my home. Knowing the only way out was through that door, I reached for the doorknob and pushed the door open.

I walked through and found myself floating in space, surrounded by stars, planets, and galaxies. I thought I must be traveling via some type of portal and had maybe come out through a black hole. I was breathing in space. That's when I saw a figure in the distance. I couldn't make out any features, but it was floating toward me. I was excited about the experience. No fear—just curiosity and acceptance.

As the figure grew closer, I realized it was my father. Why was he here? Had I shifted into a timeline where he was still alive? I had so many questions.

I rushed toward him, hugging him. He felt real.

"Are you real?" I asked.

He smiled.

"What is reality but a construct of our mind?" he replied.

"Wait, I need to understand something. Those clues, riddles, puzzles—what did they mean?" I asked. "I have so many unanswered questions."

He continued. "It's time for acceptance. Too long you've been asleep, denying the truth."

"Come with me," he urged as he took my hand.

We were suddenly walking on a brightly lit path toward a dazzling white light. The closer we moved toward the light, strangely, the more at peace I felt. The light shone with love.

I realized where I was and what had happened. The memories came flooding back. I'd never gone to the doctor. She'd never told me I was healed. I'd died of a sudden brain hemorrhage. I even remembered my moment of death, my shock, and my feeling of something being incomplete. Despite thinking that I was not afraid to die, I'd somehow refused to accept the fact that I had, indeed, died.

I suddenly understood the reason why everything happened the way it had, why I felt such remorse about the loss. I recognized who my lover was and felt an instant recognition and then a deep longing when we were separated. We were already together in the light, and I longed for it in the physical. Despite my feelings that he had veered off the path by walking away from me, he had, in fact, stayed on his path. None of it had been about romance. All of the clues and puzzles were really from my higher self to keep me on my path. I had veered so far off course because I recognized who he was. My three-dimensional self had presumed they were all the answers to a deep mystery—and they were. I was wrong to think I was searching for love, the perfect man, or the right question. The question had always been there in front of me.

My purpose. What was my purpose? The same as everyone else's—to love. And to love, we must release our fears and love others unconditionally.

That's what I'd learned in that lifetime. Having love and losing it, learning to let go, and ultimately realizing that it's not what we have in the real world, it's what we have in our hearts that matters. I would always love him. And I knew he loved me because that is the only purpose of any transcendent soul. It didn't matter what the human part of us says—we are all love.

I love myself. I am love. And will forever be love.

I was completely at peace and filled with so much love that nothing that had happened in my life mattered anymore. The life I had lived was just one life in the number of infinite possible lives. The next one would be different if I chose to reincarnate.

My father smiled.

"I understand," I said unequivocally.

As we passed through the portal, leaving the three-dimensional world behind, we dissolved into light, no longer human.

TILL THE END OF TIME

I felt the familiar light, the warmth surrounding me, and caught a brief final glimpse of my human consciousness before I passed completely into the light. I would not miss my time on Earth. I had craved the connectedness that could only be found in ascension. I was finally home.

I saw him, my soulmate. He was right beside me, as he had always been since the beginning. Lifetime after lifetime, through many struggles as physical beings, we'd tried to fulfill our mission. Decades, centuries, millennia, infinity. Starting at the very extremity of brokenness, until we finally understood, as humans, the meaning of healing, acceptance, and love. We were imperfect. Perfection was not our goal, but rather, it was to teach through acceptance of the scars and convey unconditional love of others and self. To show the way beyond the physical through to the multidimensional universe.

We had always been drawn to each other in each lifetime, not by design but because of deep recognition. We were magnetically pulled together in every lifetime, sometimes for just an instant, sometimes for longer. It was that knowing that had created the conflict within us. We'd felt the pull, but at the same time, we understood that we were meant for more than a romantic relationship. Our human selves longed for each other, but we were not meant to be together. We had known each other so long, it was impossible to keep us apart. As much as the Universe tried to intervene to prevent us from connecting and staying connected, the more we were drawn together. All those clues—numbers, birds, dreams—were to keep us on our path. Sometimes we misunderstood and strayed from the path, and other times we were blinded and failed to see the signs entirely. The message from the wild man had been clear: *You are meant for something far more important than a man.*

Our mission was complete. We had done what we could to raise the consciousness of beings everywhere, to raise the energetic vibration of the Universe. Every little action had made a difference. Earth was just one small but complicated planet. Humanity had once thrived in spiritual consciousness. But they'd been given a challenge that had brought the eventual downfall of highly ascended humans. The memory faded as time passed, and eventually most humans forgot the history and the deep connection they'd once had with the energetic realm. The higher souls could only intervene while they were present in the physical, and they would have to find very spiritually ascended humans to do their work. A difficult task that took them to the start and the finish, the infinite expanse of space-time.

Now, we were finally here together, and we merged our lights into one. We made the decision that we would no longer be apart. We would not live separately in the physical world again. We would be united forever.

They were there at the beginning, and they would be together at the end, as time looped upon itself, infinitely flowing.

I am the Alpha and the Omega.

We are one.

UNITED IN LIGHT

The man looked at me with confusion.

"Wait," he said.

"If this story is about you, how did you get back here and remember?"

"That's a story for another time. But I promise I'll tell you as soon as I come back again," I replied.

The monk understood.

I waved goodbye and continued down the path from the monastery on the Tibetan mountainside. I smiled. I'd thought I'd never come back again, but it's so much easier when you return knowing your past and your future, and you don't have to work alone. We would accomplish so much together. Imminent changes were coming to Earth.

"Are you ready?" I asked.

"Always," he replied.

"It's time," we replied together.